SERVING
HIM

SERVING HIM
SEXY STORIES
OF SUBMISSION

EDITED BY
RACHEL KRAMER BUSSEL

CLEiS
PRESS

Published in the United States by Cleis Press, Inc., 2246 Sixth Street, Berkeley, California 94710.

Printed in the United States.
Cover design: Scott Idleman/Blink
Cover photograph: Vasko Miokovic/Getty Images
Text design: Frank Wiedemann

First Edition.
10 9 8 7 6 5 4 3 2 1

Trade paper ISBN: 978-1-57344-925-0
E-book ISBN: 978-1-57344-942-7

Contents

INTRODUCTION: LUCKY NAUGHTY GIRLS

I'm so lucky to have such a naughty girl like you in my lap," Jake tells Deirdre in "What You Deserve" by Lori Selke, the opening story in the book you're about to read. In many ways, that sentence, its promise and passion, its claim and command, is what this book of kinky erotica is all about. There are a lot of naughty girls, a lot of laps and a lot of men who understand that, in fact, they *are* lucky—whether they ever voice it or not—to have a hot, eager, filthy-minded woman eagerly awaiting the chance to serve them.

The other half of the equation, one that is vital to any BDSM story, but especially those told with an eye toward female submission, is that the naughty girls themselves know how lucky they are—and if they don't at the start of the story, they do by the end. They know they are lucky to have discovered a seed of submission somewhere within them and someone to complement and nurture that growing seed. They are lucky because they own their darkest, dirtiest desires, even the ones they struggle with, the ones that turn them on despite being taboo or unnerving in some way.

Actually, they are more than lucky; finding a master, a top, a boyfriend, a husband, a lover or simply a man who gets an essential truth about their submissive nature doesn't just happen. Well, sometimes it does, but I believe it takes a certain kind of prowess to activate and draw forth those kinds of dominants, the kind you can trust with your body and soul, your pussy and your power. What I'm trying to say is that the women here don't just wander down an alley and find a man to pin them against the wall; even when they encounter a sexy stranger, they are making a choice to obey him, to follow their own lust as much as another's command.

In "Room #3," when author Emily Bingham shuts the door on her characters, she invites us into a tale where we don't know who is touching the narrator, nor does she; we only know how much she likes it. When the narrator offers up her body, she enters into the unknown, a thrill in and of itself: "The moment I knocked on this door, I consented to become his plaything. From here on out I have no say in what will happen. No words are to leave my mouth in this space; I am at his mercy. I can only hope I've made a wise choice." In all the stories you will read here, a woman makes a similar choice, and we get to luxuriate in the ways that actively making that choice, owning up to our most dastardly, wanton, wicked fantasies can be a ticket to a ride we never want to get off.

I'm sitting in a coffee shop in San Francisco as I quote from Kristina Wright's "Coffee Break," wondering what I would do if a hot barista said to me, "Go to the bathroom now. Leave the door unlocked. Get undressed. Kneel on the floor facing the door." Actually, it's not the barista who delivers that message in her story, but it made me picture what I would do if

I were handed a steaming cup of joe and such a command.

The stories in *Serving Him* are about everything from scenes in dungeons to the ways playing with power can extend beyond what we do when we are "playing." In "Safe, Sane and Consensual," by Ariel Graham, she takes that hallmark of BDSM safety and reflects on the ways we "safeword" when dealing with polite society. "May I ask what the spanking is for?" Aaron asks Annie, and his answer just may surprise you.

There are plenty of surprises in store in this book, and whether you're a novice or a seasoned BDSM player, I hope you'll enjoy the exchanges to be found here—of dirty talk, power, roles, toys, games. These characters test each other, pushing boundaries from both sides of the top/bottom equation. Often it's the women who push their men to push them, to stop being polite and start holding them down, making them open wide, forcing them to relinquish a kind of power they are eager to let go of.

Many of the stories here are as intense as the acts described; I see them as tender, but they are likely to take your breath away, make you tremble or quiver, make you just a little bit afraid. That edge of awe and fear, of want and need, of excitement and surrender, is just where I hope these stories keep you. You don't have to be a naughty girl (or boy), in real life or in your dreams, to enjoy the twenty-two hot stories in this book, but I have a feeling they will bring out your inner naughtiness, whatever form that takes. I feel lucky to get to share them with you.

Rachel Kramer Bussel
New York City

WHAT YOU DESERVE

Lori Selke

He left me a voice mail the morning of our date. "Tonight, my dear Deirdre," he rumbled into the phone, "you're going to get what you deserve." He added a few details—a time for me to appear at his apartment, instructions to let myself in and read the note he would leave me on the dining room table, which would provide further guidance.

Jake and I had been dating long enough for me to not only have the key to his apartment but a small dresser drawer dedicated to my personal effects in his bedroom. We were an item. We only had eyes for each other. Our friends laughed admiringly at our continued chemistry.

If they only knew.

I wasn't Jake's full-time submissive. Neither of us was interested in that. But when we were together, the energy was undeniable. I wanted to please him, and he loved to put me through my paces. We'd figured out our mutual kinkiness early on and indulged it every chance we got. I'd worn a play collar for him once or twice—okay, a couple dozen times. He had toys he'd bought just to use on me. A little trust game like this one was par for the course for us. Something not too heavy, but not entirely frivolous. Serious fun.

It was a journey we'd embarked upon after one too many nights entangled together, whispering our sexual secrets to each other in the dark. Somehow it was always easier for me if I couldn't see his face when I made my true confessions. He had noticed how turned on I got when he pulled my hair, yes he had; when he slapped my ass once or twice, or held my head down on his delectable cock. He liked to watch me blush when he trailed his fingers along my jawline. The rest felt as inevitable as gravity.

If I was ever supposed to be ashamed of my submissive desires for Jake, then I must have cut that class in school.

I rushed home after work and quickly showered and changed my clothes. Jake's voice mail hadn't left any specific instructions as to my attire.

So I dressed for myself. I put on a casual dress with a black crossover top and a pretty black-and-white graphic print skirt—it always made me feel like an old-time, pre-Technicolor movie star. Black bra, black panties, bare legs, men's-loafer-inspired pumps. Kind of like what I'd wear to the office, only a little bit funkier.

Jake worked in customer support. He liked it partly because nobody ever saw his face—or his shoulder-length hair, or the tribal tattoos on his forearms, plus the one on the web between his left thumb and forefinger. He'd had a dissolute younger life that he'd only begun to divulge to me, but he'd reined it in when he started to go gray at the temples. Suddenly health insurance became a priority, too, and the debauchery could wait for the weekend.

Or nights when I slept over. Whatever worked.

I let myself into his apartment as instructed. And also as instructed, I found and read the note on his little two-person dining table, which was bare except for a slim little dog collar I was so very intimately acquainted with already, as well as a blindfold, one of those ruffled satin sleep-mask styles. This one was pink. The note simply said, *Put these on.* So that's what I did. First the collar, then the blindfold. Then I carefully perched on the edge of the dinette chair and waited.

He must have been waiting down the hall, perhaps in his bedroom; I heard his footfall on the carpet. He'd taken his shoes off. I straightened my back, hands in my lap, already squirming with anticipation. But instead of feeling his touch or hearing his coarse whisper close to my ear, I heard the clanking of pots in the kitchen, then the gentle chink of china on the table next to me.

The first words he spoke to me were, "Open your mouth." So I did. He slipped something inside it, to sit on my tongue. "Taste it," he said. It was salty and tangy and sweet and creamy and chewy. Eventually the sensations sorted themselves out. Half a fig, stuffed with goat cheese and sprinkled with thyme and honey, he told me as I chewed. He gave me another. I licked leftover honey off his fingers.

He continued to feed me by hand—slivers of lemony roast chicken, slices of cheese, cubes of bread, olives, room-temperature cherry tomatoes that popped in my mouth. I tried not to giggle or bite the tips of his fingers, but it was hard. It was hard to hold still and let myself be fed. But when I got too fidgety, he just said, "If I have to, I'll tie your hands behind your back." I stopped fidgeting.

"Slow down," he said again after a few more bites. "Savor it. We've got all night. Don't worry, I guarantee you're going to get what you deserve."

At that phrase, I pressed my thighs together and swallowed another bite. Carefully. He put a straw to my lips. I sucked in cool water. I tried to concentrate on the flavors and textures in my mouth, on the press of his fingertips when he wanted me to open, but suddenly the image of Jake dressed as a severe schoolmarm, ruler in hand, spectacles teetering on the tip of his nose, popped into my head. I tried to suppress the giggle starting to burble up from my throat and failed.

"Are you laughing at me, young lady?" he purred, right next to my ear. It didn't help. Another terrified giggle escaped me. And then I was stuck in a hysterical laughing fit. "I'm sorry," I managed to mumble between giggles and gasps for air. "I'm so sorry, Sir, I'm not laughing at you, I'm just laughing, I can't help it." I forced the last word out. "Mercy!"

In response, I heard the low rumble of Jake's own laughter. "Mercy? For what? I haven't done a thing to you yet except feed you dinner. Are you telling me you're ready for dessert?" I could feel him move away thanks to the breeze of cool air against my ear where before had been his breath, hot and moist.

The tines of a fork pricking my lips prompted me to open again and accept a bite of strawberry cake. With strawberry frosting. And another. And another. At some point he switched to feeding me with his fingers again and soon I was licking crumbs off his fingers and he was smearing frosting on my cheeks. I started laughing again and said, "Uh-oh."

He put a frosting-smeared finger to my lips to shush me. "Never apologize for laughing," he said. "Even at me." I could almost hear the smirk I knew had to be gracing his face right now. "I think you're done with your dessert," he called from somewhere in the kitchen. "Now it's time for mine."

And that's when I realized my panties were wet.

"I heard how you called me Sir." That hot breath was back,

tickling my ear. "We never negotiated that, you know." He kept his finger pressed against my lips. "Don't apologize. I know you. I know you want to. But I don't want you to. So hush. Hold still. Listen."

I held still. I could hear him shift his body next to me. There was a pause. Then I found myself pulled roughly into his lap and tipped over, my butt in the air. He pushed up the skirt of my dress but left my now-damp panties in place. "You're not gagged," he reminded me, "and I expect you to let me know if I should stop for any reason. Now," he said as he wound his free hand in my hair, "what was that about calling me Sir?" And he smacked my ass firmly with his open palm.

I yelped. He smacked me again. "Well?" he said, and punctuated his question with a third blow.

"I don't know, it just slipped out!" I cried, sounding embarrassingly hysterical already. Suddenly there were tears threatening in the corners of my eyes, and it was getting hard to breathe through my nose. Jake just kept swatting my butt with a steady, slow rhythm. "Don't apologize," he warned me, and I burst out sobbing instead. He slowed his spanking pace, but he didn't stop.

"I'm flattered that you chose to call me Sir, sweetie," he said in his smoothest of tones. "That's not why I'm spanking you. You haven't been a bad girl. You're a good girl. You've done everything I've asked so far. And you're going to get what you deserve." He punctuated his last sentence with a pounding blow. "But not yet. I'm spanking you because I like it, not because you deserve it." He rubbed my sore ass for just a moment with his hand. "You like it, too, though, don't you? Even though you're crying."

"Yes," I whispered.

"Just a little bit," he replied. "I can tell. Your panties are soaked." He smacked me right between the legs, cupping my vulva, to emphasize his point. I yelped. He hit me there twice more. "I'm so lucky to have such a naughty girl like you in my lap. A girl who likes it when I spank her." *Smack.* "Who gets wet when I spank her." *Smack.* "This girl here in my lap, she's going to get exactly"—*smack*—"what she deserves." Three more smacks, and then he pushed me roughly to the floor.

"Get on your hands and knees," he said. His voice was turning rougher, hoarser. "Stick that bright red butt up in the air." I scrambled to comply.

He pulled my panties down.

I felt the shock of air hitting my wet, wet pussy and I wanted to crawl away, hide under the table, except that I was still wearing the blindfold and wouldn't be able to see where I was going and would surely hit my head on the table leg or something stupid and embarrassing like that. I knew the sight of my bare ass in the air was nothing Jake hadn't seen before. But before, I'd always been able to watch him watching me. Now I couldn't see anything at all. Was he scrutinizing my last pubic hair trim job? Noticing some strange deformity I couldn't even see?

Was he laughing at me? All eager and spread and unable to see?

I sat there on my hands and knees for a moment that kept stretching out like taffy. Why didn't he do something? I strained to hear the sound of a belt buckle releasing, a zipper being pulled down. I heard nothing, for too long. Then, too far away, a plastic clink. He was putting something on the table. A brush to spank me with some more? Some other nefarious toy?

Then I heard the buzzing.

"Remember when I asked you to masturbate for me?" he asked.

I blushed. It had only been a week or two ago, and it was one of the hardest things I had ever done. Also one of the hottest. "Yes," I said, biting back the almost-automatic addition of "Sir." What was wrong with me?

"Well, I took notes," he said. "So I think you might appreciate this." And he pressed whatever was making that buzzing sound gently up against my clit and started making slow circles with it.

I struggled to keep my butt in the air, my legs spread wide enough for him to reach his target. "Hold still," he said in his low grumble. "Let me do the work." So I held still, and my knees trembled, and my whole body flushed. "Tell me when you're getting close to orgasm," he said. "Tell me if I need to stop, or change up. Talk to me, Deirdre. Tell me how it feels."

I hated him for one hot second. The last thing I wanted to do right now was think in words. I wanted to melt blissfully into the carpet beneath his hands in a puddle of moans and soft sighs, but the bastard was making me talk. He'd probably ask for full sentences. He wasn't going to get them. "That feels good," I managed to say between increasingly rapid breaths. "Don't move. Don't stop."

He chuckled. "All right." And then he slapped my ass. "Keep talking. Tell me what you like. Tell me how it feels when I touch you. When I tell you what to do."

"It makes me so hot. You're making me so hot. Oh, I want you. I want your hands, I want your cock, I want you to keep doing that to my clit. I want you to take me, use me. Oh, god, I can't believe I just said that. Please don't make me beg. I hate begging, I hate talking, please don't make me talk any more, just let me come."

"Nobody's stopping you from coming," Jake said.

"Oh," I said, and I could feel muscles inside me shifting in response, in preparation.

"Deirdre," Jake said, leaning across my back to put his mouth near my ear again. "What do you think you deserve?"

I froze. The sound I managed to make in response was merely a whimper.

"You don't know, do you?" he said to me. I nodded mutely. "Well," he said, "I do know. You know what you deserve, my sweet little lover? Pleasure. Attention. Release. And at least one orgasm tonight. Are you ready to give it to me, sweetie? Are you ready to get what's coming to you?"

I would have laughed at the pun but I was too close to the edge. I mustered another nod of the head.

"Do you think you can come when I tell you to?" he asked.

I whimpered again. I was by now well beyond coherent speech.

"Try it for me," Jake whispered. He waited a beat, then two. Then he said, still in a soft voice, "Come for me, Deirdre. Give me your orgasm. Show me what you can do. Come get what you deserve."

And when he spoke those words, the crest of the wave I was riding broke. My knees buckled. My hips started rocking against Jake's hand, and I moaned as I collapsed sideways onto the carpet. Jake moved with me, keeping his hand between my legs, deftly switching off the vibrator and cupping my pussy as he arranged himself next to me, spooning me. I shuddered beside him. I could feel myself slick with sweat and pussy juice, and I smelled the tang of my come in the air.

Jake started stroking my hair. "Wow," he said. Then he pushed the blindfold off my face and kissed me gently on the forehead.

"I think I might need some water," I managed to croak after a few minutes.

Jake laughed. "No, honey. I think you *deserve* some water."

And he got up and moved to pour me a glass from the sink. I watched him, bleary with satisfaction and utterly spent. He squatted next to me and lifted my head so that I could drink. "Let me go get you a towel," he said after helping me sit upright. "You deserve that, too."

"And a bath?" I said, trying to sound sprightly. "And some chocolate cake?" I blinked at him with wide, wide eyes.

He laughed. "Don't push your luck." Then he helped me up off the carpet and down the hall into his warm, soft bed.

COFFEE BREAK

Kristina Wright

I wait for him to call with the impatience of a hungry cat waiting for the mouse to peek from under the stove. Except in this case, he's the cat and I'm the mouse, waiting for him to pounce and put me out of my misery.

There are six files open on my laptop and a dozen emails that all require my immediate attention, but I repeatedly check my cell phone to see if he has called in the thirteen seconds since I last checked it.

He makes me wait on purpose. He likes torturing me like this. He calls it anticipation, not torture. He says he likes the way my voice sounds breathless when he's kept me waiting for so long I can barely contain my impatience. Or my excitement. Or the wetness pooling in my panties—if I'm even wearing panties.

The phone rings as I pick it up to check it for the hundredth time in thirty minutes. I'm so startled, I drop the phone and it skitters across the slick tabletop. I catch it as it slides off the edge.

"Hello?" My voice is as breathless as he always says it is. It would piss me off if I weren't so excited.

"Are you thinking about me fucking you?"

That's what I love about him. There's no preamble, no chit-chat. He cuts right through the bullshit and gets to what he wants. What we both want.

I laugh, but it's the kind of laughter that's an escape valve for all of my pent-up frustrations and nervousness. "Something like that," I say, conscious of the people around me.

"Tell me."

Damn. I should have known he wouldn't let me off the hook just because I'm in public. I cup my hand around the phone and whisper, "I'm thinking about you fucking me."

"Louder."

I glance at the woman next to me, who is wearing ear buds and seems oblivious to my presence. "I'm thinking about you fucking me," I say, louder this time.

Maybe too loud, because she glances over at me with a weird expression on her face. I turn my head to the wall, but the full-length mirror reflects the three tables of people behind me, not all of them wearing ear buds.

"Good girl," he says, his voice silky smooth. He sounds like sex. He *is* sex. "I want you to go order a coffee."

I look at the cup in front of me, nearly untouched. "I already have a coffee."

He makes a sound of impatience. I know that sound too well. It means I've displeased him. If he were here in person, there would be some punishment to go along with that sound. I can't decide whether I wish he were here or not.

"I want you to order something specific," he says. "A medium coffee with cream and two pumps of vanilla. Because you're as far from vanilla as they come, aren't you, Meredith?"

I nod, even though he can't see me. There is nothing vanilla about me except the way I dress. I'm your typical coffee-shop freelancer, dressed for comfort, not for style. "Yes, Sir," I say. "Then what?"

"You'll know what to do. What's your safeword, Meredith?"

"Latte," I say. It was my choice of word—a tip of the hat to my love of coffee. "Will I need it?" I can't imagine what he's up to, but a shiver of anticipation tickles along my spine.

"I hope not."

Ah. There it is. The expectation that I will be able to handle whatever he is about to do to me. He pushes me, this man I've grown to love and lust for. Pushes my limits, pushes me to test my own boundaries. I say yes to everything he wants because I know I'm really saying yes to myself; yes to the secret desires and longings that I've kept bottled up for too long. Yes to the need I have that bubbles to the surface whenever I hear his voice.

"Go order your coffee, Meredith."

"Yes, Sir."

"And Meredith?"

"Yes?"

"I wouldn't have you do anything dangerous or anything that I didn't think you would enjoy," he says.

"I know." I *do* know. I trust him.

"Good. Talk to you soon."

He hangs up before I can say good-bye.

I pack up my laptop and tuck my phone into the side pocket of my messenger bag. The coffee shop had been quiet when I got there an hour before, but now it was hopping with the lunch-time rush. I wait in line, impatient as the woman in front of me asks the difference between an espresso and an Americano. I nearly groan in impatience while she confers with her friend over which to order.

Finally, it is my turn. The barista is a young hipster guy with black-rimmed glasses and the perpetual smirk of coffeehouse workers.

"Could I get a medium coffee with cream and two pumps of vanilla?"

The smirk is replaced with a genuine smile and an arched eyebrow. "Yeah?"

I bite my lip. What does this guy know that I don't? "Um, yes."

"Just a minute."

I am distracted by a group of moms pushing strollers in line behind me. Barista guy clears his throat to get my attention. "Here you go," he says, handing me a cup that feels suspiciously light. "It's on the house."

"What? Oh, thanks," I say, wondering what I am supposed to do with the cup. I start to ask him, but he is yelling to the guy at the end of the counter.

"Hey, I'm past due for my break. I'll be back in fifteen."

"Excuse me? Are you done?" asks one of the stroller moms behind me.

I nod and move out of the way, carrying my empty cup to a new table since the one I vacated has been taken over by two businessmen with BlackBerrys.

I turn the cup in my hands and see that it is marked, *See inside.*

Curious, I pop the plastic lid off and look inside. A piece of paper is folded up in the bottom of the cup. I fish it out, unfold it and read it. Then I read it again, a feeling of dread sitting heavy in the pit of my stomach.

Go to the bathroom now. Leave the door unlocked. Get undressed. Kneel on the floor facing the door. Masturbate to orgasm no matter who walks in. You may get dressed and leave when you are finished. Then call me.

My breath catches in my throat. I feel like I am going to hyperventilate. I refold the paper so I won't have to look at the words. But not seeing them is worse somehow than reading them, so I spread the paper out on the table and read it again. The businessmen walk by on their way out and I instinctively cover the paper with my hand as if they might read my secret shame.

I remember what he said on the phone. He wouldn't have me do something dangerous. He wouldn't have me do something that I wouldn't enjoy.

But how can I enjoy *this*? It *is* dangerous. He is pushing me too far.

And yet...I cannot resist him. Even though his commands are written, I can hear his voice in my head. That makes it easier somehow to obey his words.

I refold the paper and tuck it in my pants pocket. I stand on shaky legs and make my way to the bathroom carrying the empty cup. Out of habit, I push the button lock on the door once it closes behind me. Then I remember his command and twist the knob so the lock pops free. I stare at the door, waiting for it to open. It doesn't.

I put my messenger bag on the floor and take a breath. It does nothing to quell my nerves. I figure the sooner I get this over with, the sooner I can leave. Once in motion, I move quickly. Shoes, socks, pants, blouse, bra, panties, until I'm standing naked in the coffee-shop bathroom.

I'm loath to kneel on the dirty floor, so I pull a handful of paper towels from the dispenser on the wall and lay them out on the floor. Then I kneel, facing the door. I take another deep breath. How the hell am I supposed to masturbate like this? I'm not even aroused.

I slip my hand between my thighs and discover otherwise.

I'm soaked. My pussy feels swollen and my clit is rigid between my fingers. I am so nervous, I hadn't realized I am turned on. But of course he would say I am turned on because I am so nervous. Because he is pushing me to my limits. Because it arouses me to be humiliated like this, to risk being caught, to think of a stranger walking in and catching me kneeling on the floor and stroking myself to orgasm.

I am already ridiculously close to orgasm. This won't take long. I close my eyes and think of him standing over me, watching me. I slide my fingers between the lips of my engorged pussy and thumb my clit at the same time. *Two pumps of vanilla,* I think. My perfume I dab on my wrists is vanilla scented and the smell wafts up to me—the scent of vanilla and my own sweet musk. Cream, he said, and I feel my own cream trickle out as I stroke my G-spot.

God, he knows how to get to me. He knows just the right words to drive me wild.

Head thrown back, eyes closed, I pinch and pull my nipples, feeling them tingle and burn as I manhandle them roughly, the way he would. My clit throbs in response, aching for the same rough treatment. I pull my fingers from my pussy and rub my entire mound, grinding against my palm as I pump my hips up to meet my hand. I'm so close.

I'm panting and my pulse is pounding in my ears, but I hear the distinct click of the door opening. I freeze, midthrust. For a split second, I hope it's him. I hope he's come to watch me obey his commands.

I open my eyes and see the barista smirking at me. I panic. He locks the door behind him.

"I—uh—I," I stammer, but there is no explanation. I'm kneeling naked on the bathroom floor of the coffee shop, a puddle of my own juices underneath me. What can I say?

"He gave me a fifty to come in here," he says, fumbling with his belt and unzipping his pants. "But I'd do it for free. You're so fucking hot."

His dick is hard and thick and beautiful. I swallow hard. Fucking him wasn't on the agenda. I can't. I won't. I realize I'm shaking my head before I can even say the words.

"I'm just here to watch," he says, stroking his erection. "Don't worry. If you want me to leave, just say latte."

He knows my safeword. I feel the panic fade. He won't hurt me.

My hand is still pressed between my legs and as I watch him touch himself, I find myself matching him stroke for stroke.

It doesn't take long. He leans against the door, his eyes fixated on my hand between my legs. He occasionally glances up my body to watch me torture my tender nipples before going back to my fingers pumping my pussy so hard the wet sound echoes off the walls.

"Yeah, do it," he mutters, and I doubt he even realizes he's speaking. "Do it. I'm watching you."

And I'm watching him. Watching the way his dick swells as he masturbates, watching as his body goes stiff and the first spurt of come hits the floor two inches in front of my trembling knees. His eyes close as he comes, but I can't look away. I want to see him.

Then I'm coming. Coming as he jerks off in front of me, for me. Instead of feeling helpless and at his mercy, I feel like a fucking goddess being worshipped.

"Look at me," I hiss between clenched teeth. "Watch me come."

His eyes flutter open as he slowly milks the last drops from his dick. He is breathing hard, his forehead glistens from his exertion, but he watches me. Watches as I stare at his dick and thrust three fingers inside of me, watches as I open my mouth in a silent moan and imagine the taste of him on my tongue. I pump my fingers inside my pussy, feeling wetness trickle over my knuckles. I come until I am trembling and whimpering and barely able to remain upright. Finally, I close my eyes.

When I open them a moment later, he's gone. The door is unlocked again, and though I'm weak as a newborn deer, I hurry to stand and lock the door before I dress. Moments later, I'm splashing water on my face to cool the heat in my cheeks. I exit the restroom, eyes straight ahead, afraid to look behind the counter and see if I'm being watched.

"Have a nice day," someone calls after me, but I'm pretty sure it's not the same barista. I don't know where he's gone, but I know he won't ever forget this experience. Neither will I.

Out on the busy street with people hurrying past on their way back to work after lunch, the whole scene feels surreal. Standing at a light on the corner, I squint in the sunshine and press REDIAL on my phone. He answers on the first ring.

"Did you enjoy that, Meredith?"

I let out a breathy sigh. "That was intense. But I can never go back to that coffee shop again." I nearly laugh at the incongruity of it. It's the only coffee shop I ever go to.

"Of course you can," he says. "You'll go back tomorrow. And you'll smile if you see him and know that he enjoyed your beauty and passion nearly as much as I do."

He's right, of course. I'll go back. I'll do anything he wants me to do. Because when all is said and done, it's all about me and what I need and want, even if I can't find the words to say it.

CHATTEL

Errica Liekos

S hortly after they got married, Alex had told Sasha, "Do what you want. I love you, and I don't ever want to stop you from being you. If you want to be with me, be with me. If not, don't. I won't stop you. I want you to be happy."

Her friends thought it was romantic. A man who wasn't jealous, who didn't get weird about girls' night out, or get mad when she wanted to go to book club or knitting circle instead of serving him a beer while he watched the game. She could just do whatever she wanted, when she wanted; total freedom. They acted like it was a dream come true.

Sasha wasn't so sure.

For her birthday last year, he'd gotten her coupons for a couple's massage…for her and a friend. She took Lucy. The year before, it had been tickets to the ballet, with a suggestion that she take Regina. He hated the ballet, so she did. He knew she didn't enjoy softball and didn't ask her to come with him when he played. Once they even went to a movie theater and split up to watch different movies when they couldn't agree on documentary (him) or action (her). She did all the things she would have gotten to do if she was still single.

Sasha was miserable and hadn't a clue what she was supposed to complain about. She tried talking to some of her friends about it and ended up getting lectures on women's rights and the history of marriage.

"Women used to be chattel," Lucy scolded, "and you're telling me you want your husband to be *more* possessive of you? What next, you're going to take his last name?"

"Fine, you can trade husbands with me," Regina said. "I'll take the man who wants us to see *Swan Lake* and you can have the man who tells me I put the 'bitch' in 'Stitch-and-Bitch' every single time I leave the house for knitting circle. You don't know how good you've got it, honey."

Sasha didn't want to give up her maiden name, and she didn't want Alex to turn passive-aggressive on her, but yes, she thought, she did want him to be more possessive. Maybe he *should* demand that she show up to root for him at his softball games, and maybe he should make her watch the movie he wanted, just because he wanted it, and wanted her company at the same time.

So when she opened her latest birthday present over dinner at a Turkish restaurant to find a pair of opera tickets, she couldn't keep quiet any longer.

"I don't want to keep going to these things alone."

"What do you mean?" Alex said. "There're two tickets."

"But you don't want to go with me."

"So you should miss out on *Don Giovanni* because I don't like it? Come on, who's that girlfriend of yours who's into opera, too? Lucy? Jessie?"

"It's Lucy," said Sasha. "Jesse is a guy. You want me to take another man to the opera with me?"

"If that's who you want to take, I'm not going to stop you."

Sasha slammed her hands down into her lap in frustration,

knocking her napkin to the floor. "I want to take *you*. But I know you don't like opera, which means my choices for enjoying *your* birthday present to me are to make you miserable or be without you. Doesn't that seem a little wrong to you?"

Alex leaned forward, crossing his arms on the table. "Okay. Tell me what's going on."

"It's just that...marriage is compromise, right?"

"It doesn't have to be."

"Yes, Alex, I think it does. I can't do all the things I did when I was single and still be the kind of wife I want to be. Or have you be the husband I want you to be." Sasha trailed off. Alex's expression was unreadable.

"Go on."

"You're so focused on us each doing our own thing." Her voice dropped to almost a whisper. "Sometimes I feel like you don't really want to be married to me."

Sasha didn't order her usual dessert, and Alex skipped his coffee. They drove home in silence. Sasha felt like crying. Regina was right; she had the perfect man, and she didn't appreciate him. He'd dressed in his best suit, given her a chance to wear a new dress, taken her to a lovely dinner, and bought her a present that showed he thought of what she liked at the expense of his own preferences. And now he was pissed off at her, and she'd ruined everything.

Alex used his key to open the door to their apartment, then stepped aside to let Sasha enter first. She stepped into the dark, intending to turn on the hallway light, but Alex closed the front door before she could reach it. She felt his hand close around the back of her neck, stopping her forward movement. She stumbled, and his other arm wrapped around her waist and caught her. She felt his hot breath as he began to speak, close and low, into her ear.

"Maybe I haven't been making myself clear," Alex said. "I let you go because I trust you to come back. Men like me don't give away things they're unsure of. But maybe you haven't understood my confidence in you."

"I..." Sasha started to speak, but Alex's hand tightened behind her neck, and she stopped. He rubbed his five o'clock shadow against her throat then continued.

"I can see now that I made a mistake," he said. "You don't need your freedom, do you? You need to know you're wanted. You need to know you're loved."

Sasha felt her legs go weak. She leaned on Alex, and he held her weight. There were no windows in their front hall. She opened and closed her eyes to the same solid black.

"I'll be clear from here on out. You're mine. I own you. I tell you to spend time with your friends because it gives me pleasure to do so. Because I like you missing me, and I like it when you come home with new stories from your friends and your world to entertain me. I expect you to stay independent and entertaining to me. Do you understand?"

Sasha nodded.

"Because I have no interest in owning something weak and unchallenging, Sasha. I want you strong, and I want you to have your own interests." Alex lowered his voice even more. "But you belong to me. Do you understand?"

Sasha nodded again.

"I'm not sure you do. Go into the living room. I'm going to show you."

Alex released her, and she walked deeper into their apartment, less sure in her heels than she'd ever felt before, sensing his body just a few inches behind her with every step. She turned the corner, and their living room appeared before her, lit by the streetlamps shining through the windows. She hesitated at the doorway.

"The middle of the room will be fine."

Sasha moved to the center of the room, and hesitated again.

"Face me."

She did. Alex had his arms crossed, but his body language didn't seem closed off. There was a trace of a smile dancing around his lips.

"It really is a lovely dress you're wearing," he said. "Take it off."

Sasha blinked then did as she was told. A pile of green silk quickly landed in a puddle around her feet.

"And matching underwear, too. Lovely." Alex stepped forward and ran a hand along her side, like he was calming a skittish horse. "But I want you, not some fancy outfit. Take them off as well, if you please."

The courtesy of his phrasing somehow made the words even less of a request, more of a command. She unhooked her bra and let it fall. She slid down her panties and stepped out of them, then nudged the clothing away from herself with one foot, so she wouldn't trip on the fabric. Sasha looked down at her high heels and back up at Alex.

"Shoes, too?"

He chuckled. "Let's not go nuts."

Sasha stood in front of her husband, naked except for three-inch black leather heels. He was close enough to touch, close enough that she could grasp him with both arms and cling to him for reassurance, but she didn't dare. She held still as he watched her, his eyes roaming over her body, finally meeting her eyes.

"Good girl," he said.

She shivered.

"Oh," Alex said. "I see. Let's warm you up." He knelt down in front of her, reached for her hip and kissed her.

Sasha had never really liked anyone, even Alex, going down

on her. It made her self-conscious. Without thinking, she stepped back.

Alex stood up faster than she realized was possible, grabbed her upper arm and yanked her body back toward his own.

"See?" he said, pressing against her. "This is what I'm talking about. I'm not doing this for *you*. This is what *I* want." He took her other arm in his hand as well and started walking forward, forcing her to walk back. Each time she took a misstep in her heels, his arms supported her. "You belong to me. All of you. I don't care if this makes you nervous, I don't care if you don't understand how beautiful and delicious I find you." Sasha took a final step backward and felt the fabric of their couch against the backs of her legs. "Now lie down, spread your legs and give it over."

Sasha felt the heat and moisture building between her legs. She did as instructed.

"Better," Alex said. He knelt again between her legs, lifting one up onto the back of the couch, knocking the other so her calf hung over the edge and her shoe rested on the floor. She felt his breath and then his tongue on her lips and clit, and she moaned.

"Behave yourself or I'll tie you down," he murmured, and went back to work, alternately licking, nibbling and sucking on the sensitive flesh. She tried to stay quiet for him, but soon enough was moaning in a different way. Her self-consciousness was gone. He wasn't doing it because he thought he had to. He wasn't trying to impress her; he was trying to devour her. His tongue slid all the way inside her, then out again to investigate her folds. She had no obligations other than to be his toy, and this knowledge changed the entire experience for her. She felt the couch getting wetter and wetter beneath her and knew that it wasn't his saliva that was the culprit. She moaned again and started thrusting her hips into his mouth. When her legs started to quiver, he stopped.

"Not yet," he said. He stood and backed up a few steps. "Kneel."

Sasha pulled herself off the couch and sank to the carpet in front of him. Her head was level with the bulge in his pants.

"Take it out."

Sasha unfastened his belt, unzipped his fly and lowered his pants just enough to release his cock.

"Suck me," he said. "No hands."

Sasha gently closed her mouth over the head of his cock and began working up and down the shaft.

"Suck harder," he said. "Not faster, just harder. That's it. Let it almost come out of your mouth, then take as much as you can."

Sasha tried to oblige, but after only a few strokes, she let him slide out of her mouth altogether. She reached up to put him back, and Alex caught her wrists.

"That's too bad," he said. He sounded amused. "I said no hands." Sasha opened her mouth, but he cut her off before she could get a word out. "I believe I also said that if you didn't behave, I'd tie you down."

Still holding her wrists in one hand, he stripped his belt out of the loops on his pants with the other. He bent down and placed the belt against her lips.

"Hold this."

Sasha looked into her husband's eyes. What she saw made her open her mouth, then close it obediently over the leather.

"Good girl," he said again, and she knelt up straighter for him. He put her hands behind her back then held out his free hand for the belt again. She bent her head down and dropped it into his palm. He leaned over her and tied her hands behind her back with the belt, sliding it through the buckle until it was tight on her wrists, then looping the excess leather through the center and closing her hands over her own restraint to hold it in place.

The tail of the leather hung down along the crack of her ass and on her ankles before coming to rest on the floor.

"Very nice." Alex tilted his head near hers and smiled gently. "Your nipples tightened up again. It's so obvious that you like this, I can't imagine why I didn't do it before." He straightened up, and his cock was in her face again. "Try again."

Sasha did. She sucked with the strength and speed Alex demanded, and she bobbed her head to chase after his cock, regaining her suction as quickly as possible each time after he slid from her mouth. She felt the roof of her mouth pressing down tight on him, and reveled in the noises her throat made as it grasped and released him. Alex reached for the back of her neck, slid his hand up into her hair, then closed his fist on a huge handful of her mane. Sliding out was no longer a risk as he pumped her head up and down his shaft, steady, strong and fast, until he moaned himself and came, holding her tight and still with his cock deep in her mouth, shooting down her throat as she struggled to swallow and suck and breathe all at once. Slowly his grip on her hair lessened, and she withdrew.

"That," Alex said, "was perfect." He tucked himself back into his clothing, refastened his pants, then hooked his hands under her arms and stood her up. Then he spun her around and released her wrists from his belt. "But we're not done. I believe," he continued, as she turned back to him, "that you were interrupted earlier." He gave her a little push, and she landed on the couch with a bounce. "It's your birthday, so I'm going to make it easy for you." He pressed her shoulders down onto the cushions and spread her wide apart. Then he took her hand and placed it between her legs.

"Show me," he said. He undid his tie and wrapped it over her eyes, plunging her into blackness again. "Let me know when you get close."

She couldn't remember ever being so wet before. Her finger circled her clit, and it barely qualified as friction. She began using her whole hand, and soon the feel of Alex's fingers on her nipples and his breath on her thigh pushed her over the edge.

Sasha gasped. "Now," she said. "Now."

Alex bent to her clit and drew her into his mouth. His tongue was her world as she came.

The next day, Alex came home with another package wrapped in birthday-patterned foil. Sasha opened it and found a thin, soft, black leather collar with a small ring in the front. Her eyes widened.

"Where did you get this?"

"Never mind," Alex said. "I got it, and that's enough." He took the collar out of her hands and showed her the metal loop built into the buckle. Then he pulled her into the bathroom and in front of the sink so she faced the mirror. He stood behind her, and she watched while he fastened the collar around her neck.

"The buckle can be locked," he said, "but for now I'll trust you to wear it when I tell you to. You'll take Lucy to the opera this Saturday, not Jesse. And you'll wear this all evening until you get home. You can put it on yourself, but I'm the only one allowed to take it off. And next time, you're going to need to ask permission to come. Do you understand?"

Sasha nodded. She felt the heat growing between her legs again as she leaned back against her husband and raised one hand to stroke the leather and hook a finger into the collar's ring. She smiled, wondering if Alex had already bought a leash to clip on to her collar, and wondering how exactly she was going to conceal the collar from—or explain it to—her friend Lucy.

UNDER DIRECTION

Teresa Noelle Roberts

The package was hefty for its size, and oddly shaped, wrapped in sleek, dark-red paper neatly enough that I suspected Luke hadn't done it himself. "I brought you a present," Luke said. "Actually it's more I bought myself a present for you to use."

The wording, and the fact it wasn't near my birthday or any holiday, made me suspect a sex toy, or lingerie, or some other bit of erotically charged fun. I made quick work of that pretty wrapping.

But this toy wasn't anything I expected.

"A Feeldoe?" I raised one eyebrow at the alarmingly turquoise contraption: two conjoined faux-cocks, one end to insert into me and the other, obviously, for someone else to enjoy. Turquoise *is* my favorite color, and it certainly looked like it would be fun in the right, meaning female, company, but I wasn't seeing any immediate application. "Who's the lucky lady you imagine me using this with?" We were basically monogamous, but we'd never ruled out the possibility of adventure if the right opportunity arose. Maybe this was Luke's not-too-subtle way of saying he'd found what might be the right opportunity. "Or is it more flexible than it looks? I'll try anything once."

Luke smiled one of those smiles that always wiped out some of my fears while firing up a new crop, much more fun than the originals. I felt a stirring in my groin. "No, girl. You'll be using it on me."

It was not couched as a request. Luke was using his dom voice, which was way more Barry White than his normal intonation and had a Pavlovian effect on me.

My stomach flip-flopped, and my heart fluttered in a funny way. So did my pussy, but the little jolt of arousal at the unexpected order was squelched by a wave of mixed feelings. "Wait a minute," I said, thinking maybe I was missing something important, like Luke was joking but I didn't quite get the joke. "Did you say what I thought you said? That you want me to use that thing on you?"

His naughty grin broadened and he got that look that said he knew he was pushing me and it was making him hard to see me squirm. "You're going to fuck me up the ass. How do you like that?"

My heart had gone from fluttering to outright thumping, and the butterflies in my stomach had turned all Cirque du Soleil and were doing backflips, launching off my spleen. Words swirled in my head: *hot...scary...what the fuck...I can't...hot...wrong...* but I couldn't make them into anything like a coherent answer.

Luke stepped behind me; his big, muscular body pressed close to mine; his hardening cock jutting against my ass. His voice dropped to a low, menacing whisper that thrilled through my clit, even while my mind was swimming in a well-known river in Egypt. "Answer me, girl." He wrapped his arm suddenly around my throat, pressing just enough to create an illusion of danger that my hindbrain didn't realize was just an illusion. I felt myself melting, in the thrall of his dominance, but it didn't help me answer his insistent whisper, "How do you like the idea of fucking me up the ass?" If anything, the hormonal haze made my thoughts more scrambled.

I had to say something. He'd demanded an answer, and with him in this mood, I couldn't disobey without consequences. (The consequences wouldn't be bad, might even be fun, but I hated knowing I'd merited a "punishment," however mild.)

I forced the word salad in my head into something that was at least a sentence, if not a coherent one. "I can't do that!" I squeaked. "It wouldn't be right."

"Why not?" Not a trace of Barry White there. The last time I'd heard Luke use that hyper-reasonable voice, he'd heard someone say the president was a vampire and was trying to figure out if the speaker was rhetorically challenged or just bat-shit crazy. Still, his hard cock pressed against me, the warmth of his body surrounded me and he still had his arm across my throat, so it was kind of a mixed message.

The reason why not seemed obvious to me, but he wanted me to spell it out, so I did. "Because you're a dom! Subs get ass-fucked, not doms." My logic felt unassailable as long as it was in my head, but once I said it out loud, I wasn't so sure.

"That's greedy." He eased up on my throat and moved so he could look into my eyes and pull me close. "Why should subs have all the fun?"

I blinked. "I'm not supposed to do things like that to you. Demeaning things. Controlling things."

Luke laughed and kissed my forehead. "Is it demeaning when I do it to you? I always thought you liked it. If you're just going along with it because you know I enjoy it and you're a

good girl...well, I should know that. It can be fun to push you
sometimes, but I want to know I'm doing it."

I think I sputtered. "It doesn't feel demeaning with you, not
unless you're playing the naughty-little-slut game, and then it's
a game and it's hot. And I definitely like it. It makes me feel like
a bad girl in a great way, and I come really hard from it."

"Not so different from why I like it."

"But it feels so controlling when you do it to me."

He laughed. "That's because I'm me and you're you. You love
to be controlled in bed, and I love controlling you." His voice
dropped back to the panty-drenching Barry White register.
"Which is why I'll be guiding you every step of the way when
you fuck me—as a service to your dom."

I melted at that. I whimpered. "I'm scared," I whimpered,
my voice very small. "I've never done it before."

"I have," he said, "and I'll tell you what to do." He pulled me
close and stroked my hair as I trembled with a combination of
relief and outrageous need.

When the time came, it still seemed wrong to see Luke ass-up on
the bed, his knees drawn up under him. I could imagine him as
a great cat crouching, preparing to spring. I wanted to imagine
him preparing to spring, to leap on me and take me down hard,
to bring this night back to a place where I was comfortable—to
a place where I might be hurt, might be embarrassed, might be
entirely out of my own control and under Luke's, but where
I never felt any sense of doubt about the rightness of what I
was doing. I'd always been more comfortable bottoming, but
with Luke, in the face of Luke's dominance, the preference for
yielding had become a need.

Now he wanted me to fuck him with a dildo, to do something that had always seemed very take-charge during my

experimenting-with-women phase back in college. I was shaking as I knelt behind him on the bed. "I'm scared," I said. "I don't think I can do this. I know I don't *want* to do it."

"I can smell your arousal from here," Luke said.

"It must be from before." We'd spent a long time kissing and cuddling, to get me relaxed enough to try this. That must be why I was aroused, not from the idea of fucking my dom in the ass. I knew some women liked that sort of thing, but it had always been alien to my fantasy life.

"Touch yourself," he ordered. "Slide your fingers into your pussy."

The order jolted through me. I obeyed, even though I expected dryness, resistance. Instead I slid into slick, gripping heat and let out a hiss of surprise and pleasure.

"You're wet, aren't you?"

"Drenched," I admitted in a small voice. My touch had made me aware my cunt was wet and swollen, but still it seemed to be happening to a different woman in another country. My brain was in such a tangle that I could barely let myself feel the arousal. "I don't know why."

"Because you're a good girl. Now smear some of your juices on my asshole."

I tensed up, afraid of hurting him. "Won't you need lube?"

"Do what I say. I'll tell you when I need lube."

At the hint of sexual menace in his voice, my pussy clenched again and I went from drenched to full flood. My fingers trailed a thread of slick wetness as I pulled them from myself and touched them to him. To his asshole.

I wasn't entirely inexperienced at exploring the male butt-crack, but I'd never had a lover who was really enthusiastic about the notion, so my explorations had never gotten too far. I touched the pinkish-brown wrinkled opening gingerly, not because I was repulsed, but because I wasn't sure how much pressure I should use and it seemed better to err on the side of caution.

"You're slick," he said in a growly voice. "Feels good. Now circle." He kept making small, pleased noises as I did. The noises gave me confidence. I must be doing something right.

"More of your juices." I complied, noticing to my dismay— or was it delight?—that I was wetter than ever, and I couldn't help stroking my clit, just to tease and ease, before I got back to work on Luke.

"Now ease the tip of one finger in." He hissed when I obeyed, and I feared I'd hurt him until he groaned, "Yeah. In and out now, gently." My breath caught in my throat, but I did it. He was tight around my finger, gripping, hot, a little rough. Not like fingering myself—no natural lubrication to speak of and so very tight, though he was easing up readily. What was most jarring to me was that touching him like this was arousing me, maybe because he was so obviously enjoying it.

"Lube," he grunted abruptly. I'd had the bottle of lube in a bowl of warm water on the nightstand—I hate cold lube and I couldn't imagine Luke would like that startling feeling any more than I did. It still felt chilly on my hands, but my efforts to warm it up in my palm and transfer it provoked a "just squirt some on me!"

I cracked open, and waves of love and lust widened the cracks. I hadn't been looking forward to doing this, and I was still weirded out. Being the person doing the penetration felt powerful on some primitive level, and I wasn't entirely comfortable feeling powerful in relation to Luke during sex. But doesn't the person providing the pleasure always have some power, even if she's submitting? Luke's urgency, the way he moved as I squirted and then stroked the lube, reminded me that if I was taking him, it was because he wanted it that way. As I eased my finger into him, I said, "I understand now."

"Good girl." It sounded like he spoke through clenched teeth. "Deeper now..." And sooner than I expected, "Try another finger."

This time my pussy clenched shamelessly as I obeyed him, working a second slicked finger into his slick passage. I'd never done this before. I'd never wanted to do this before. But it was starting to feel right.

Luke coached me through opening him up, readying him. I wasn't confident I'd actually found his prostate—my fingertips couldn't detect what the research I'd done told me I might feel. (Yes, I'd done research. If Luke insisted I fuck him, I was determined to do it well.) But the way he reacted told me I was doing a good job.

Finally the moment I'd been dreading arrived, the moment he said, "Get the Feeldoe and put it in you. Then lube. Lots of lube."

Only I found I wasn't dreading it as much as I'd imagined. For one, the turquoise contraption felt good, filling my wet pussy and pressing against my clit. Whoever designed this thing was some kind of twisted genius. And Luke obviously wanted the feeling of having his ass filled, stretched, fucked. I loved pleasing him, making him come. This was just another way to do it and damn, the way the toy was made, I might even get off myself.

Still, I was nervous. I'd practiced thrusting into a pillow so I wouldn't feel like a complete klutz, but a pillow didn't have nerve endings.

I positioned myself to enter him and froze. The toy looked huge from this angle, although it was smaller around than Luke's cock, which filled my ass in a wonderful way. "Are you sure? I asked, and I'm not ashamed to say my voice was shaky.

"Go slow," he responded. "I'll tell you when you should speed up."

The first inch or so was agony—for me, not for Luke. I imagine it was mildly uncomfortable for him, because the first bit of butt-sex usually is, but from the noises he made, it was an interesting discomfort, the kind he knew would sort itself out to pleasure. But until he thrust himself back, taking more of the silicone dick than I would have dared to give him, I was one scared sub, convinced I was going to damage him.

Luke knew his own body, his own desires, and quickly I was as much a toy as the dildo. I was fucking him, sure, but mostly he was fucking himself, working the turquoise dick in and out of his ass.

My universe realigned. Everything made sense again. I was fucking him, but at the same time, he was using me for his pleasure, a configuration I found erotic as well as comforting. Okay, make that using me for both our pleasures. As he moved—and as I saw how he took charge even with me sticking a dildo into his ass from behind—the Feeldoe's evil, awesome design worked its magic on me. As Luke moved and I pumped my hips to keep up with him, the toy moved as well, pressing on my clit, tormenting and tantalizing me. Pleasure spiraled through my body. My cunt gripped the toy. My hands gripped Luke's hips. "Stroke my cock," he ordered, an edge of delicious desperation in his voice that didn't dampen the aura of command.

I crashed forward onto him as I obeyed, and lost some of the leverage I needed to keep fucking him. He more than made up for it, though, moving fast and hard, fucking himself through me. My hand worked double time.

"Now," he cried, then, "Yes!" and then he gave a shocking roar that might have started out as an English word, but was no longer recognizable. His big body convulsed and shook. Hot come shot out, filling my hand, splattering onto the bed.

With what seemed to be his last scrap of energy, Luke said, in a voice hoarse with shouting, "Good girl. Good, obedient girl. Come now."

With a little help from my come-slick fingers, the sated pride in his voice pushed me into my own moment of incoherent screaming.

Once we'd cleaned up (and by cleaned up I mean a few swipes with some wet wipes and dropping the Feeldoe in the upstairs sink to be dealt with later), I said, "That may never make my top ten list of favorite things to do in the sack, but I could definitely get used to seeing you come that hard, and hearing you say 'Good, obedient girl' in that dreamy voice. I liked knowing I was pleasing you by doing something I wouldn't have even imagined trying if you hadn't wanted it. I guess I'm even more of a sub than I realized."

Luke let out a rumbling, throaty chuckle, like Barry White might laugh if his partner did something delightful and unexpected. Through the laughter, he said, "That was the point: to let you know you and I are reaching a new level of D/s, one I don't think either of us expected when we got together."

"That and you like being fucked in the ass sometimes." Sub or not, I'm still human, and wiseass remarks still pop out of my mouth.

"That, too," he agreed. "Why should you subs have all the fun?"

THE LETTER

Tiffany Reisz

By their thirteenth date, Brice decided to just make a game of it. Would it be tonight that Leigh dumped him? Tomorrow? Would they make it to fourteen dates? Fifteen? Why she kept saying yes to him when he asked her out was beyond him. On their second date they'd kissed. On their fourth date, they'd made out on her sofa. After that, all progress toward consummation came to a screeching halt, entirely without explanation.

Dinner came. They ate it. Dessert came. They ignored it. Brice studied Leigh over the top of his wineglass. Beautiful girl...red hair with streaks of brown and black, dark eyes that brightened with laughter. She had a freckle on her top lip that he loved to bite when she let him kiss her. On date twelve she hadn't let him kiss her. Tonight she wouldn't even look him in the eyes.

"Are you a virgin?" Brice asked, deciding he had nothing to lose at this point. Clearly things were going nowhere. If he couldn't have her, maybe he could at least get some answers.

Leigh sat up straighter and gave him a look of profound shock.

"No...of course not. Where—?"

"Born-again virgin? Incredibly Catholic? Do you have an STD? HIV? Raging antibiotic resistant tuberculosis? If so, I'm willing to work around any and all of that."

Leigh laughed nervously and shook her head.

"Brice, I don't have—"

"Why haven't we slept together yet?"

She sat her glass on the table and crossed her arms over her chest.

"It's complicated," she began, then stopped. "I wish I could explain. I want to but when I try, it's..." She brought a hand up to her lips and pulled at the air as if trying to drag reluctant words from her mouth. "I can't."

Her body sagged, and suddenly she looked so small and sad in the chair across from him that he wanted to drag her into his arms and apologize for even bringing it up. This girl...he fucking adored her. Her laugh, her smile, her dry sense of humor, the way her voice went all goofy and high-pitched when she played with his dog. He had to have her in his life. And she must have felt something, anything for him, to keep saying yes to all these dates. So why...?

"Can't what? Can't tell me? Can't explain? Can't say it in any language other than French? That's fine. I'll learn French. Just tell me."

She shook her head.

"I should never have said yes to the first date, Brice. And I'm sorry. The kind of person I am, I don't need to be meeting guys at the gym and going out on regular dates. It doesn't usually work for people like us..."

She paused and growled, as if profoundly frustrated with her own inability to explain. Brice wondered what the hell she meant by "people like us."

"I like you so much that against my better judgment—" she continued.

"Oh, thank you very much for that."

"That's not what I mean." Leigh clenched her hands and groaned softly. That groan—he heard passion in it. Frustration. No way was this woman frigid. Exhaling through her nose, she looked up and met his eyes. "You're the nicest guy I've ever met. You're kind and sweet and chivalrous and gentle…"

"Horrible, I know."

"I'm not like you. I'm different. And I want to tell you how but I just can't."

"Then write me a damn letter if you can't say it."

Leigh's eyes widened at the suggestion.

"A letter? I can do that. I'll do that."

"You will?" He hadn't been serious. But the thought of a letter, the thought of any form of explanation for her strange behavior, excited him. At this point the thought of knowing why she wouldn't sleep with him turned him on almost as much as her actually agreeing to sleep with him.

"Yes. I'll write it and mail it to you. It'll explain everything. And then you won't have to see me again once you know. You'll just know. And then we'll both feel better."

Brice nodded in agreement.

"Fine. Write the letter. But I promise you will see me again."

Leigh turned her head and stared down at the floor. She grabbed her sweater from the back of her chair, threw her purse over her shoulder and stood up.

Looking at him, she gave him a wan smile.

"Read the letter first. Don't promise me anything until you do."

And with those ominous words, she left the restaurant and maybe even his life.

For the next three days, Brice rushed home from work and checked his mailbox before doing anything else. Nothing... nothing...nothing. Finally, on day four, he held it in his hands. Pale pink envelope, black ink...the letter.

It took all of his willpower not to open it up and begin reading it right on the sidewalk. Shoving it in his pocket, he went inside, poured a glass of white wine, sat in his favorite chair and carefully sliced open the envelope.

The stationery matched the envelope—black ink on pale pink paper. Scanning the first page, Brice saw no date at the top, no "Dear Brice." His eyes fell onto the first sentence and he began to read.

Naked, she waited on the bed...knees to her chest, arms around her shins, head bowed and eyes closed. As instructed. As always. And as instructed she'd pulled her long hair into low pigtails that hung over her shoulders and tickled her collarbone. He seemed to love the combination of sweet and spice in her—her hair so girlishly arranged, her body naked, her eyes rimmed with black eyeliner in full Cleopatra mode. Anything he wanted she would do for him. She'd style her hair as he wanted, dress as he liked...anything for him. All it took was an order.

She stiffened slightly when she heard the bedroom door open. Closing her eyes tightly, she fought the need to look at him. God, she loved to look at him— at his black hair, slightly unruly, his bright blue eyes, the leather bracelet he wore along with his leather-banded watch. He'd always rolled his shirtsleeves to the elbows. Until Brice, she'd never realized how erotic male forearms could be.

Brice paused in his reading. He looked down at his shirt. As usual he'd rolled his shirtsleeves up to his elbow. On his left wrist a black leather bracelet accompanied his leather-band watch. He ran a hand through his black hair, a few inches longer than his mother considered entirely respectable.

Wait...was Leigh writing about him? No way. They'd never... only in his dreams.

Brice kept reading.

She inhaled sharply when his hands came to her shoulders and rested there for a moment. From her shoulders they slid higher until he held her by her neck, his fingers lightly pressed into the hollow of her throat. Her entire body came alive at his touch, both gentle and threatening. His hands fell away from her and then it was his lips on her neck instead.

He trailed kisses from her ear to shoulder and back up again. She flinched as his teeth met her earlobe.

"Hands and knees," he ordered in a whisper. Without hesitation, she rolled forward and into position.

His hands traced a path down her back, over her hips, down and up her thighs. His fingers found her labia and he opened the delicate folds wide...wider... She knew he was looking at her and studying the most private parts of her. Her skin flushed, but not with embarrassment, only with desire.

He pushed two fingers into her. He went deep until he

found the core of her. A small sigh escaped her lips as he
pulled his fingers out.

Then all the gentleness disappeared.

With one hand he forced her onto her chest as he
yanked her arms behind her back. Cold metal ringed her
wrists—handcuffs. He pulled her roughly up to her knees
and dragged her to the floor.

"Knees," he ordered, and she went down without hesitation. He opened his pants, took her by the chin and
forced himself into her mouth.

She loved the size of him, the feel of him in her mouth,
the slight salt taste of him against her tongue. Slowly,
he thrust in and out while she sucked and caressed and
kissed. Ostensibly she was his property. At moments like
this, however, she knew she owned him as much as he
owned her.

His breathing quickened and she readied herself to
swallow. Instead he pulled out of her mouth, grabbed her
by the shoulder, and dragged her once more to her feet.

"You enjoyed that, didn't you?" he rasped the words
in her ear.

"Yes, Sir."

"Because you like sucking cock? Or because you like
sucking my cock?"

She smiled.

"Yes, Sir."

He laughed softly and nipped at her neck.

"Good answer."

She stood still and waited as he undressed. She wanted
to watch, wanted to see him, but kept her eyes respect-
fully lowered to the floor. Only her respect for him, for
his dominance, his mastery of her, eclipsed her love and

desire for him. Everything primal and female in her wanted to lay itself at the feet of everything male and primitive in him.

Brice coughed and adjusted himself. He took a large drink of his wine and considered turning the air-conditioning up in the house. Suddenly it had gotten incredibly warm in his living room.

With a hand on the back of her neck, he steered her to the closed closet door. As a birthday gift to her, he'd gotten an over-the-door restraint system. Now he had somewhere to tie her up. Made for much easier flogging.

He took off the handcuffs and tossed them aside before forcing her arms over her head. One by one he buckled her wrists to the straps on the door. She turned her head and rested her cheek against the cool painted wood. In and out she breathed, slowly, deeply. She let herself fall into a meditative trance that even the first fall of the flogger on her back didn't interrupt, but the second, much harder lash did. She grunted with every new strike. Her back burned with pain. Her body burned with need. She wanted it to go on forever. She needed it to stop immediately.

He dropped the flogger and pushed his chest into her back. At first she flinched from the pain, but the feel of his warm body on her ravaged back sent renewed desire singing through her skin.

When he unstrapped her from the door and pushed her onto the bed, she felt only relief. At last.

"Stomach," he ordered, and she rolled over and spread her legs. She loved to spread for him, to offer her body to him and let him take her any way he wanted.

Straddling her hips, he pushed inside her and started to thrust. Underneath him she lay almost motionless as he used her body for his own pleasure. He clamped his hands over her wrists and pinned her hard against the bed as he moved harder and faster inside her. She tried to ignore how her body responded to his every movement, his every touch. The tip of his cock grazed her G-spot and she gasped into the sheet. His mouth caressed the sensitive center of her back. She wanted to raise her hips and take him even deeper inside her, let him make her come. But this time was for him and him alone. She loved to give herself over to him, to be used solely to satisfy his own needs. His breathing grew louder. His grip on her wrists tightened to the point of pain.

"Bite," he ordered and she brought her mouth to his forearm and dug her teeth into his skin. With a long shudder he came inside her as her mouth continued to mark the occasion on his arm.

He exhaled and she relaxed back into the sheets. She hadn't broken the skin but he would have a beautiful bright-red bite mark on his arm for the next week. Knowing him, he'd take a picture of it and email it to her tomorrow with a little note that confessed he grew hard every time he looked at the bruise.

With casual strength, he flipped her onto her back. He kissed her breasts, sucked lightly and then harder on her nipples. Gripping her knees, he forced her legs wide open and pushed two fingers into her again. His fingers moved easily inside her as wet as she was with her arousal and his semen. A third finger joined the other two. The shock of pleasure sent her hips rising off the bed. He turned his

hand inside her and pinned her back down against the
mattress as he brought his lips to her clitoris. With his
hand he rubbed her G-spot, massaged her labia, moved in
and out of her with spiraling circles that sent her reeling
while his lips and tongue tasted her, explored her, brought
her to the edge and left her hovering there. Finally he let
her fall off the edge but caught her before she landed.

He kissed his way up her stomach, over her rib cage,
across her chest and up to her lips. Their mouths met
finally and she tasted herself on his tongue.

Pulling up he gazed down at her and brushed a tendril
of hair off her forehead.

"My Leigh," he whispered. "Mine."

"Yours, Sir..." she sighed and closed her eyes.

Brice reached the end of the letter and immediately started over
reading it from the beginning.

So this was her? This woman who wanted to be owned, used,
flogged, tied up, taken, possessed...this was Leigh? This was the
woman who hadn't even slept with him after two months and
thirteen dates? This wildly sexual, confident, erotic woman?

I'm different...those were her words at dinner. Brice shook
his head. The woman had told him no not because she was a
virgin or religious or scared, but because she was kinky and
needed to be with someone like her.

*You're the nicest guy I've ever met. You're kind and sweet
and chivalrous and gentle...*

Leigh was kinky and she thought he wasn't. And that's
why she hadn't gone to bed with him in all this time. For
weeks she'd wanted to tell him what she was, but she'd been
too embarrassed, too shy. And even now she hadn't told him.
She'd shown him instead. And from the almost painful erec-

tion pressing against the fly of his pants, it was clear he'd liked what he saw.

In seconds, Brice was out the door and in his car. Racing across town, he made it to her apartment in record time.

He pounded on the door and Leigh answered it with wide, wary eyes.

"Brice...what is—?"

Before she could finish the sentence, he clamped a hand over her mouth, stepped inside the apartment and kicked the door shut behind him.

Shoving her against the wall, Brice locked his legs against hers, immobilizing her.

"Don't scream," he ordered as he lowered his hand from her mouth. Already she'd begun to breathe heavily. Sliding a hand between their bodies, he reached under her skirt, pushed the fabric of her panties aside, and slid a single finger into her. She burned against his hand, already wet for him. "Still think I'm too nice for you?"

She swallowed.

"No."

"That was you in the letter." He moved his finger in and out of her as she began to pant. "But you didn't name him. Was that me? Or your dream man?"

A slight smile played at the corner of her lips.

"Yes, Sir."

Brice brought his mouth to her neck and bit her hard enough to make her whimper. He hoped she had nowhere to go tonight. He didn't plan to let her go until dawn.

"Good answer."

RUN, BABY, RUN

Vida Bailey

The sunlight shone through the glass lemonade jug and danced watery patterns over the tray she carried out into the garden. The first thing Lana saw over the rise of the hilly lawn was her two-year-old son, Billy, flying into the air. He hung for an instant, dark against the blue sky, then plummeted earthward to be caught in two strong, outstretched hands.

She cleared the crest of the hill and found her husband and son tangled in a laughing heap on the ground. Their daughter Katie launched cushions at them from a safe distance. The two kids looked up and saw her setting the tray down on the table. Billy extricated himself from his father's grip with violent wiggles, and they both ran for the drinks and snacks.

"We're playing chasing!"

"Daddy was chasing us! I was flying!" Jason rose to a crouch and looked in their direction.

"And I'm coming to get you again…" The kids ignored the threat, and Billy raised a peremptory hand.

"No, Daddy, we're having our snack. Chase Momma instead."

Lana's eyes cut to Jason, noting the shift in his posture and the light in his eyes—still mischievous, but more intense than the laughing shine they'd held a minute before. Beneath the sleeve of his black T-shirt, his tattoo danced as the muscle flexed a little.

"Okay. Get ready to run, Momma."

"Jay, no, wait, don't!" But Lana was already out of her shoes and gathering her skirts at her thighs. She tensed, legs braced, her heartbeat loud in her ears, spiky adrenaline skittering round her system. He stood and watched her. She knew she didn't have a chance, but she was still compelled to try. For a second, she'd be safe until she moved. She let the muscles in her legs find their way, push her forward at just the right time. As the soles of her bare feet flexed on the grass, her eyes sought out an escape route, then returned to his. When they made contact, Jason made a move toward her, and she took off.

Lana's legs pumped under her long layered skirts, and her head flew back in panicked laughter as she felt him catching up with her. It was too late for any long sprint; she had to feint and duck and try and get the picnic table back in between them. Her heart thudded and her breath caught. She weaved around and made for the table, but she could feel him behind her, quiet and sure. With a whoop, Lana felt herself tackled and her breath running out as he bowled her to the ground. She landed safely on the soft grass, his body lean and hard along hers as her chest rose and fell against him. Her pulse was slowing, pounding against Jay's fingers where he held her wrists above her head. The alarm faded into relieved, excited heat as the fear-flight hormones left her bloodstream and she wiggled a little in delight at being held down against the grass.

"Are we playing Kiss Chase?" he asked, breath hot on her heaving neck, a far cry from the innocence of playground games. His crotch pushed against her a little, and he ducked his head in for a quick kiss.

"Aw," she complained, "you're not even out of breath."

"All my excitement's on the inside, baby," he grinned, then hopped up and held out a hand to pull her upright before the children could descend on them in a pile-on. Lana leaned into her husband's shoulder as they walked back to the table, felt his hand drop lightly to her ass and smiled as she poured the kids' drinks.

It had been years, now, since Lana had been caught. One day the escape had been too panicked and careless and the car she'd been fleeing in brought her to an abrupt, violent stop. She was tangled in twisted metal and sirens and pain. There would be no running, just learning to walk again. For that, there was Jay. With a smile and his calm. When it was time to walk, he still smiled, but there was no taking no for an answer. He didn't seem to feel sorry for her at all, he just kept pushing her. *Yes, it hurts; yes, it's hard; yes, you can.* And when she cried and said it was all pointless because she was going to be locked away anyway, he just shrugged and said, "Well, you'll still need to walk out of the place when the time comes." So she would shut up and do it. And when she got out of jail, walking on her own two feet, he was there.

The sun had sunk, the children lay in bed: one sprawled above the covers, one curled tightly beneath them. Lana woke to night song, cicadas and the babble of the river reaching through the clear air. Jay was gone, his side of the duvet turned back. A note on the rumpled sheet glowed white in the moonlight. Lana read, rolling one corner against the pad of her thumb, and for a second she scrunched into a ball and hugged herself before leaving the bed.

The lights were off as she descended the staircase, but the hall was lit by the brightness from the full moon. It shone on Lana's silk nightgown, making it seem to ripple like water against her belly and thighs as she moved down the stairs. It was a delicate pale green, the color of the calla lily where it just begins to shade from petal to stem. Closer inspection showed it to be scarred in many places with fine lines of tiny stitches. Lana loved the silken rasp against her smooth calves as she moved, a near silent sound, echoed by the whisper of her hair against her shoulders, her soft thighs sliding together as she walked.

On the hall table lay a tiny key. Slowly, Lana picked it up and closed the silvery coldness of it into her hand, a flash of ice against her hot palm.

Make for the trees, the note read. Make for the trees. That was all it said, but Lana knew more or less what to expect. She shivered as she walked barefoot across the kitchen floor. Her nipples were already pushing against the slippery fabric of her nightgown before she opened the door to the cool breeze. She leaned for a moment on the door frame, seeking a last moment of calm before she stepped outside and tried to let instinct take over. She knew he'd give her a head start, but that wasn't so much a kindness as a psyche-out.

She looked out across the darkened lawn, bleached to silver in the moonlight. The trees were a solid line of black at the other end of the garden. Somewhere in between them was her goal, or at least a hiding place. Once she stepped onto the lawn, she would be a baby gazelle until she reached the trees. Where was he watching from? The garden was full of shadows, too many spaces for a man in black to melt into, to observe unobserved.

Okay. It was time. If she took too long he'd come and get her. She didn't want that. One, then two delicate barefoot footsteps across the gravel. A couple more, slip slap on the patio flags, and then her feet were cooling in the dew-rich grass. She shivered. Anticipation and fear were jostling each other inside her, one making her wet in spite of the other or maybe even because of it. She felt her pulse beat in her pussy, in the hardened flesh of her nipples, in her throat.

She heard the opening bars of the song about her beautiful life that she always played in her head and counted down until the chorus exploded into life, sweeping her into a sprint as it did so. Her feet were sure on the slippery leaves of grass, toes digging into the soft turf. The breeze blew her long, thick hair back out of her face and cooled her hot skin. She could feel sweat forming and drying away instantly in the warm night air. She kept her eyes fixed on the entrance to the small wood at the end of the lawn, navigated the hill safely and bolted toward it. She was doing fine, growing into her stride, her heart balancing the exertion with the tension of waiting for the attack. She'd waited too long to move though. Before she was halfway across the grass, a dark, lithe figure peeled away from the shadows to her left and sped toward her. She could see him running hard, straight for her, as if he had no intention of stopping. She fought the panic, her breath hoarse in her ears, and skidded to a halt just before he reached her. She was down on one knee as he fought to stop his headlong rush. As he struggled to turn and grab her at the same time, she hooked his ankle with her outstretched leg and swept his feet out from underneath him. Black gloved hands groped for her ankle from where he sprawled on the ground, but she planted her foot square on his abdomen and pushed herself off to the satisfying sound of the wind leaving his body. That would slow him down.

It did, for seconds. She didn't stop to look back, but hammered toward the trees, the key tucked safely and burning hot into her palm. She pumped her legs, feeling the strength in her thigh and calf muscles, relishing the small singing pain as she pushed against it. She was so in love with herself when she ran. Her tits were annoying her, though, bouncing so free, unsupported by the silk. She'd wanted a sports bra, was even ready to negotiate a bandage, but he'd looked at her with laughing incredulity. Reaching to stroke and cup the curve of her silk-covered breast, he'd raised his eyebrows. "Seriously? Lycra, and *this*?" Lana saw his point, but she resented it now, as her boobs bounced around with a liquid rhythm of their own, threatening to spill out of the silky bodice. She heard fleet footsteps behind her again, and put an extra push on, the fear of being chased, of being caught, edging up another notch. It filled her chest, closed in her breathing space as she felt him get closer.

Damn, she thought. *Maybe I shouldn't have stood on him.* There was no way she could outrun him on the straight, she knew. *Make for the trees.* The phrase beat with the pulse in her ears, in each rasping breath. Five more steps, then two, and she was in the dark space beneath the summer leaf canopy. The path felt warm beneath her feet after the dewy grass. She ducked into the shadows and looked around. They had to be somewhere easy to see.

Jay always gave her the key to the cuffs, and a fair chance. There was the tacit understanding that whoever got to them first got to use them on the other. In truth, Lana couldn't really imagine what she'd do with Jason in cuffs, though sometimes her mind did slide to interesting possibilities. But not while she was running. Right now there was just the chase, and escape, and getting to the goal, and all the beautiful things that the safe fear did to her insides. Listening intently for breath, or footsteps, she craned around again, searching in the light spaces between the shadows for the cuffs. And then she saw them. They were hanging by a cord from their favorite tree, actually over her head, out over the path. Too high to stretch up to. She knew she could climb for them and reel them in, but she could also feel the hands that would grab her as soon as she tried to pull herself up into the tree. So, what—a run and jump? A stick? She'd be right out in the open. And why was he being so quiet? Was he waiting for her next move?

She decided to go for it. Swiveling around, she took a step out onto the path, and weighed up the distance out of the corner of her eye. A running jump should do it. Her eyes squinted, trying to pierce the darker shadows. She stood still, as her brain put puzzle pieces together, and she strangled a gasp as she realized that the darker shape in the shadow she was looking at was Jay. He was standing right there, a few feet away, looking at her! She froze. No point running now. Lead him away, double back? Ah, she knew there was no way out other than to act, to move.

She took a few steps backward, softly, so as not to startle him. Had he noticed her seeing the cuffs? She had to go now, before he moved, or she'd be out of space. She took a breath, two quick strides, and jumped, arms outstretched. She felt her fingers graze the soft leather of one dangling cuff, and then Jay's hard body hit hers, a collision that flung her onto the soft layer of leaves and pine needles beneath her with a thud, knocking the air from her chest when she bounced between the ground and her husband. She writhed and gasped underneath him and tried to kick free, but she didn't really get anywhere this time.

Jay laughed softly.

"Gotcha." His lips moved against her ear as he whispered and the tip of his tongue traced a path up her neck and into her ear. He blew lightly on the wet trail of his saliva, and she shivered. The fight in her was always swallowed so quickly once he was back in control. Desire and deference were lit in its place. Jay peeled himself off her and pulled Lana to her knees.

"Hands behind your back." She complied and bent her head. "Don't move." Lana knew she had the option of springing up and running again, while he was loosening the rope the cuffs hung from, but that would change the rules a little and the languorous thrill of submission had already started honeying through her veins. From the corner of her eye, she could see the baby monitor clipped onto his belt, and the flogger tucked in beside it. Her cunt clenched and she shut her eyes.

Deftly, Jay buckled the cuffs onto her wrists, and, sliding the key from her clenched fist, clicked the little padlock closed between them. He walked back around in front of Lana where she knelt, and stroked a thumb down her jaw, then pushed it against her lips.

"You can run, little girl, but you can't hide for shit." She smiled, turning her head and nuzzling the side of her face into his palm. She kissed it, her eyes closed, waiting for the sound of his combats opening, the smell of his sweat in her nose. His cock stood out from his body elegantly, statuesque in the moon-light and shadow. His hand in her hair turned her toward it, and she leaned in, loving the feel of its heat against her cool face. She opened her mouth on his shaft once, resting her lips against him, then licked from base to tip before he angled her head back farther, and she opened and took him in. On her knees in the dark, in the wood, with her hands bound and throat filled, Lana's mind grew sweetly blank. She wasn't anxious, or grateful, she simply *was*. Maybe the awareness that she would soon be bent over or bound naked to a cool trunk and whipped as soundly as Jay wanted made her wetter between the legs than his hand in her hair or his cock in her mouth had done already, but it was hard to say. There was the wind in the trees, the noise of her mouth on Jay's cock, and *her*. Alive, strong, free.

Jay pulled Lana off him, and she opened her eyes blearily. He pulled her to her feet and ghosted his fingertips down the backs of her captive arms to jingle the lock on the cuffs.

"Want to run away?" he whispered in her ear. She looked up at him from under her hair and shook her head. No more running, at this stage. She was happy where she was.

The trees in their wood were made for them. Jay unlocked Lana's cuffs and stretched her arms above her head, clipping them to a rope that hung waiting from a branch. He kissed her neck, traced the lines on her stomach that he once said he could see mapped in silver in the moonlight. She shivered under his touch and waited. The nightdress must be torn again. It might be time to go looking for a new one. The whisper of the flogger sliding out of his belt brought her back to her stretched arm muscles and she waited for its touch, a sweep across her shoulders, her back, her ass. She lowered her head when it stung, the blows falling fast, not the heavier strokes she preferred. With a squeak, she twisted away from a smack that wrapped around her ass cruelly. Ah, this was the retribution—not the flogging, just *this*. She pressed her face to the smooth coolness of the trunk she was tied to, pressed her hips against it, let the tree absorb the blows for her. *I am the tree*, she thought for a second, and felt her sap rising, her connection to the earth.

Did Jay see how far away she was getting? All of a sudden the toy landed on the ground beside her, his hands were on her, lifting her legs. He hooked one over the branch to her right and held the other one in the crook of his own strong arm. His clothes were open already, and she yielded to the push of his cock when he stroked against her once, twice, spreading her wetness, opening her seam. And then he was inside her, stretching her, not quite waiting for her to catch up with him. His thrusts pushed her roughly against the tree trunk but she didn't complain, because her clit was getting crushed against its solid bark and Jay's fingertips were baring her breast roughly, slapping and kneading it. He shoved against her and buried his face in her neck. He slowed a little, lifting her higher to take some of the strain off her arms. Wrapping both arms round her thighs and hips, he pushed a hand between the tree and her hot, wet skin. She ground onto his fingers and gasped.

"Jay! I'm going to come, I can't..."

"Not yet, honey, hold on a second, wait, now."

He slowed a little, stilled his fingers. He gave her a chance to inhale the night air, heavy with blossom and him, but then the monitor on his belt crackled, and he started to work her faster, taking no chances, thrusting her hard against his hand and the tree. She was sacrificed, hung on the tree for him, stretched. She was the ache in her arms and the pounding in her cunt, she was tree bark and widespread limbs fixed where he chose, for his pleasure. This sent her spinning out of herself and into an orgasm that wracked through her and dissolved everything into green-black sky.

When Lana came back to herself, she found she was sitting on the ground, leaning against Jay's chest while he leaned against the tree, gently massaging the ache out of her muscles and whispering into her hair. The monitor murmured, and Jay pushed Lana to her feet. He put his arm around her and pulled her against his warm body and they walked out of the woods and back across the grass to the darkened house. Lana floated a little as they walked in sore, happy silence. She could run again now, fast but not far. She was bound to her home and her life with Jay, with bonds stronger and more secure than any she had ever known.

TACKLING
JESSICA

Maxine Marsh

I had to knock three separate times before Jessica answered her apartment door. I thought she must have been in the back, getting ready, but when she pulled open the door, she was wearing gray cotton shorts and a simple white V-neck t-shirt that plunged down between her substantial breasts. She looked like she was still in college.

We sat on the floor in front of the couch. She lay on her stomach, head propped in her hands, her bare feet absentmindedly swaying in the air behind her. Her honey-blonde hair was pulled into pigtails that made her seem younger than she actually was. She watched the football game intently, huffing when one of the wide outs missed his catch.

"So, does this count as a date?" I asked.

Jessica smiled at me over her shoulder. Something about her was acutely girlish. Fun and soft. The side of a woman that was a mystery to mankind.

"Of course it does. It's our third date."

Then she turned back to the television as though she had forgotten about me already.

I was pretty sure she had asked me over so we could screw. Why else does a woman invite you over to hang out and watch a football game? The night before, I had put my hand over hers on the dinner table. The chatter in the restaurant died down to a faraway roar in that moment—there was something there, something I could not put to words if I tried. That's the kind of moment that tells you there's a future with someone. But there was something else, something she seemed to be holding back. I could see it in her eyes. It was a personal joke to which only she was privy, and I wanted to know what it was.

The game went to commercial.

She turned to look at me again, tossing a pigtail over her shoulder. "How many lovers have you had?" she asked. Her eyes searched me as I thought. I wondered if she wanted an adjective. Many, some, a few. A number?

"A dozen or so."

She nodded matter-of-factly.

"And you?"

"Two," she said.

Only two lovers at twenty-nine. She rolled over onto her back and put her legs up on the couch, keeping her eyes on me, and then reached for my hand, brushing my fingertips with hers, making my cock stir. Fantasies of fucking her passed through my mind, pushing those little gray sweatpants down around her ankles, pinning her wrists over her head and pounding her until her heels dug into the floor and her body arched upward into mine.

"We should get tickets to a game," I said.

"I've never been."

"Never? Why not? You seem to love it."

She shrugged. "My ex-boyfriends were never into it, I guess. They never played." She thought for a moment. "Did you ever play football?"

I nodded. "In high school."

Her eyebrows rose and she sat up a little, propping herself on her elbows. "What's it like? Getting hit by big guys all the time, I mean."

The question took me by surprise. "You get used to it," was all I could think to say. "Your body gets used to it."

"Oh." She lay back again.

I got the feeling my answer bored her. Then something flashed through her eyes again and was gone in a second. Some mysterious thought, that little joke. I had the urge to hold her face in my hands and stare at her until I saw it. How could I tease it out again?

"After a while, you kind of start to crave it. The jarring. The feeling of your bones rattling inside you. It releases adrenaline, and that's addictive." That got my mind rolling, and apparently Jessica's, too, because she was staring at me again, her eyes full of suggestions I couldn't decipher. I wanted to see those big brown eyes focused on me forever, studying me, adoring me and begging me for more of whatever made her pussy damp.

"There's a moment," I said.

"A moment?" She pushed her fingers through the spaces between mine; they were entangled now. "What kind of a moment?"

"You know when they show the action in slow motion? The next time"—I pointed to the television—"don't watch the ball. Watch the moment when their bodies collide, when they first meet. There's a moment, as a player, when you blink for a second and time slows down and you feel the first contact. The adrenaline rushes to your muscles. It feels like falling, in

a way, like you're out of control and everything's up to fate."
Old memories of plays, experiences I hadn't thought about in
years, rushed through my mind at lightning speed. I wondered
if I sounded silly to her.

She smiled again.

"The good players can push through that moment. Their
subconscious or something takes over and they can make the
play come out right," I said.

"Is that how it was for you?"

I shook my head. I was surprised at how nostalgic talking
about playing made me feel. "No. I always got caught up in the
rush. I think I liked the feeling too much." I laughed, wondering
how that might sound to her. "Maybe I was too addicted
to it."

"Do you ever feel that way anymore?" There it was again.
That little devil behind her eyes. Was it stalking me?

I wasn't sure how to answer her question. These things
happened a lifetime ago, it seemed. In high school I had secretly
wondered if I was bisexual. I liked the feeling of throwing
myself into another guy. I liked the way it felt to hold my team-
mates down during practice; I liked the way their muscles
strained against my hold, especially during the real game when
I could feel the true rush of a body underneath me, wriggling
to get free, when I could hear grunting and panting and feel the
energy of pure physical will.

The warmth of her hand on my face brought me back.
She had scooted close enough so that we touched at the hip,
although she was still upside down, and her legs were still up
on the couch next to my shoulder, like a kid lounging around.
She grinned when I pushed my face into her palm.

"Are you ticklish?" she asked.

"No." No guy admits to being ticklish.

Her hand, warm and small, moved gently down my cheek and onto my chest. If it moved a little farther down she would feel my cock straining against my fly, dying to find its way into her. Before I realized what she was doing, she'd sat up halfway, reached both her hands under my arms and started to tickle me. I jostled, trying to back up, forgetting that I was up against the couch. She had me cornered, but her half-sitting, half-lying position left her unbalanced, so when I lurched forward, grabbing her hands away from me, she fell over on her side. She cried out and laughed at the same time. Soon we were wrestling.

As tiny as she was, she had some strength in her. I let her get in a few good goes at me. It's more fun to get the jump on someone when they still think they've got a chance. So I fell over on my side, too, and let her jump on top of me. She straddled my abdomen and dug her fingers into my sides, giggling and beaming as I bucked underneath her. I could have sworn she was deliberately wiggling herself against me, grinding onto the hardness in my pants, all the while tickling her way up and down my sides.

When I'd had enough I rolled us over, straddled her, feeling her shake with laughter underneath me. Her smile was huge and beautiful. I engulfed her hands in mine, pushed them over her head and put enough of my weight on her to immobilize her.

She panted, breasts heaving up against me. The little peaks of her nipples pushed through her T-shirt unabashedly. She tried to catch her breath.

"I love a good tickle fight," she said.

We panted together, eyes locked and searching one another. Burning energy passed between us, and I could have sworn she pushed her hips up into mine. With a moan I pushed back.

She went stiff and her smile disappeared. She'd had enough. I wasn't sure what I did to make her uncomfortable, but I shifted my weight to one side and slipped off her.

I felt a stab of frustration in my cock. I must have done something wrong. She got up and moved back against the couch and we returned to watching the game in silence.

Play after play and she didn't say a word, didn't even glance in my direction. Was she mad at me because I'd pinned her? I wondered if I'd scared her. Part of me had wanted to use my full-blown strength on her, but I'd held back, not wanting to seem like an asshole. Maybe I hadn't held back enough.

The game went to halftime and the players left the field, some with their heads up and others with shoulders slumping. I could relate. We sat through a barrage of advertisements before she finally turned to me.

"Tackle me," she said.

"What?"

"I want you to tackle me."

I frowned, trying to make it seem like the idea sounded crazy to me. Truly, the thought turned me on. I'd gotten pretty warmed up rolling around on the floor with her. Holding back the bulk of my strength when we played left me on edge. The muscles in my arms and legs were antsy to get some more action. I was already planning to go and run a few miles after I left her place.

"I want to feel what you were talking about before. About the moment. I want to feel that." She was earnest and direct, and it was sexy as hell.

"I could hurt you."

"So what?"

I looked at her. She somehow seemed amused and serious, at the same time.

She gave a little. "Okay, let's go in the bedroom. You can tackle me onto the bed."

I followed her to the back of her apartment, into a dark room. The shades were drawn. A small table lamp lit the room dimly from the night table next to her big, unmade bed. Her room was simple: a big bed, made up with comfortable-looking white bedding, a large dark-hued headboard and a big dresser made from matching wood. I was surprised not to see anything particularly girly. The faint smell of orchids in the air was the only feminine aspect of the room.

She went and pulled the comforter off the mattress and threw it onto the floor at the foot of the bed.

I stood in the doorway, feeling like I was on the edge of her little, private world. She positioned herself by the side of the bed, bit her lip and then looked at me.

"Okay, go."

"Wait," I said.

"What?"

"You're serious about this?"

"Yes," she said.

"Getting tackled isn't like getting pushed over or something. It's like getting hit. Really."

She frowned at me. "I didn't take you for such a pussy."

There was my little devil. I ran at her, pretty fast. I lowered my head, tucked a little and hit her, my forehead colliding with her right shoulder, my arms wrapped around her body in a big bear hug. We flew into the soft mattress. She didn't make a sound.

I pulled back to look at her, wondering if she was hurt. I was met with wide eyes, her lashes flitting; mouth wide open; ragged, hot breath passing between her lips and puffing up into my face; looking like she had just been made love to. She slowly pushed her hand between us, until my cock was cupped in her palm.

"Again," she said breathlessly.

I stood in position. I tried to think how I could hit her harder. I watched her, waiting.

She nodded.

This time I backed out of the bedroom door a little, giving myself more ground to pick up speed. I flashed back to images of training in high school, recalling hitting heavy posts during drills, hearing techniques being shouted at me, drilled into my brain and my muscle memory. I hit her again. Her body jarred, her limbs flailed like those of a dummy. This time, she gasped upon impact. The bed didn't feel quite as soft as before. She let out a little noise as I lay on top of her.

"Again."

My cock went hard.

I didn't hold back one bit the third time. That one hurt even me. The pain from the impact felt far away. A few seconds after we hit the bed, I heard Jessica whimper and begin to tremble. I looked into her eyes, watched the glossy orbs as they made an effort to focus on my face.

"Did you just come?" I asked her.

She nodded.

The scent of her wetness reached my nostrils. A raging arousal I couldn't get a hold on pulled at me. My limbs tingled from the adrenaline as I lay on top of her, pressing her into the bed under my weight, covering her small form almost completely. Usually my desire seemed directionless, aimless, out of control, but now I felt the core of me burning steadily, all of my lust concentrated on the beautiful little thing beneath me.

I lifted myself up onto my hands and knees, my stiff cock held back uncomfortably in my pants, hoping she wouldn't ask me to tackle her again. The feeling of dominating her was immensely gratifying, but at this point our little game was one of teasing. Her scent leaking through her little shorts taunted me, and I needed more.

That's when I saw it, that shadow of her inner workings peeking out at me again. I thought I had been the one teasing it out of her, but I realized that she had been calling to the fierce longing inside me. Calmness overtook her features, her body relaxed beneath me, ready to submit, ready to be a dirty little slut, ready to be *my* dirty little slut.

Breathing deeply, she spoke slowly, intently, each of her words so deliberate that I thought she must be struggling. "My last one was for three years," she said. "He taught me so much, but his cravings seemed to…dissolve over time, and he moved on. The things I wanted started to scare him."

I knelt over her as she continued. "These games can be so much about always pushing and pushing. I know how much I need, how much I want. I need to find someone who's all right at this level. Someone who can bring me right to the edge. Someone who can love me while they're hurting me."

So, the little devil behind those eyes was auditioning me. And it seemed that I'd landed the role.

Eyes loving, body limp with a mixture of exhaustion and post-climax bliss, she remained quiet while I climbed off the bed and then undressed. Her eyes found their way to my dick, rigid and jutting toward her, casting a shadow on my thigh in the dim bedroom lighting.

When I'd finished undressing, I went back to her. Instead of pulling her T-shirt off completely, I pulled it upward so that it was taut, stretched from arm to arm, covering her face. The sight of her posed, vulnerable and open to me, made my mouth water. Her tits lay exposed, the soft skin of her belly sloping delicately down to the edge of her shorts. I understood the joke now, that such a pristine body, built so delicately, so small and unassuming in personality, was meant to lie before me, like a blank canvas ready to be soiled, manipulated by someone who had the courage to take her to her limits of pain and pleasure as she desired so greatly. I watched the thin material of the T-shirt as it sucked in and out with her breath.

I tickled one of her nipples with the tip of my tongue, sucked her sensitive flesh into my mouth. She writhed as I moved to her other breast, giving it equal attention. Soft and supple skin rippled under my mouth. After I'd teased her nipples to hard, swollen peaks, I couldn't resist biting into her flesh. With each nibble, I left red marks up and down the sides of both breasts and I didn't stop until her torso was beautifully red and irritated, and she was sobbing in a tone caught somewhere between pleasure and pain. I pulled her T-shirt up from over her face, throwing it aside, and found her cheeks were rouged with arousal.

"I'm going to fuck you in the ass," I told her.

A wisp of elation passed over her face before I reached down and flipped her over onto her stomach. The little cotton shorts were easy enough to pull off, along with her panties.

"Spit," I ordered.

She complied, sending a warm puddle of her saliva into my palm. I covered my cock with the slickness, my flesh throbbing and hard as it's ever been.

"Spread for me."

She reached back, hands shaking but without hesitation, and took hold of her fair-skinned rear. A perfect, tight little puckered hole came into view. I took a moment to finger her ass until she wriggled around it, moaning so desperately I thought she might start crying.

The last step was to reach around and cover her mouth with

my hand. No point in scaring the neighbors.

At first, her little hole was so tight I thought I might not be able to have my way. Time slowed for a moment and then I felt the tip of my dick slide past the resistance and into the mysterious depths of her body. In those first moments of penetration, memories and thoughts flashed, so clear in a fraction of a second; my body hitting her body, our grunting, resistance; our bodies giving, shaken up; adrenaline, falling, out of control, her climax. The rush. Her tightness slipped around me, and she groaned behind my hand. With a generous thrust, I penetrated her up to the hilt.

Soft whines and sporadic puffs of breath escaped from the lips trapped behind my hand. She had laid her head to the side, cheek on the bed, pressed hard from the weight of my torso resting on her back. My cock burned at the sight of her eyes squeezed shut, her face fluid with pain and pleasure, twisting her beautiful girlish features deliciously.

With a shift of my hips, I began to fuck her. Her noises, like a map, guided me from long, easy strokes to a rhythm of hard, relentless pounding. When her muffled whimpering turned to deep, almost constant groaning, I reached and fingered her clit, enjoying the way her ass tightened around my cock. Tears streaked across the hand I had over her mouth, and I thought I could make out a moaned version of "Yes," which she repeated over and over as though her brain had gone to autopilot. I moved my fingers from her clit to her pussy, felt her cunt tighten around my digits. When she became silent and began to shake, like the earth moving against itself during a violent eruption, I knew she was coming.

The tidal wave of her orgasm receded, and Jessica fell limp onto the bed, jostled under my final thrusts. I came, sending a deluge of thick semen into the depth of her gorgeous ass, falling onto her back, feeling completely destroyed. After catching my breath, I lifted her fully onto the bed and lay beside her. Her heartbeat slowed, and I felt her chest rise and fall under the hand I placed in the space between her breasts. Finally calmed, with a newfound serenity, she looked up to my face and into my eyes. The little demon was gone, and her eyes were clear and calm. She was a clean slate of a woman.

SAFE,
SANE AND
CONSENSUAL

Ariel Graham

O ver the course of dinner, Annie's mother indicated there were lumps in the potatoes, that something about the stuffing in the chicken wasn't quite right and that apple pie was more suited for fall meals, didn't we think, than midwinter.

I watched Annie's face every time as she bit her lip and controlled her words, her breathing very deep, very even, very much the kind of breathing mountaineers probably do as they near base camp on Everest. I didn't think such breathing should be necessary at a winter dinner with the in-laws in Sacramento.

"Let me help you clear," I said when Elvira (not her real name, of course, but ever so fitting; Annie has never said but I'm sure her mother goes to bed at night by hanging by her toes off a rafter in the attic) finally stopped chasing the chicken around her plate and put down her knife and fork with a resigned expression.

"Yes, perhaps that would be best," Annie's mother said.

I saw Annie tighten her lips and look to her father, oblivious as ever.

I opened my mouth—slowly, not sure what I was going to say—and Annie, imperceptibly, shook her head, then said, "Aaron?"

I stood, as always almost hitting my head on the chandelier over the dining room table. We only eat here on those endless nights Annie's family comes to tear into the carcass of something formerly known as their daughter. I mean, of course I mean, on the nights they come to dinner.

I picked up my plate and more or less rocked Henry's plate out from under his utensils, which he still held poised. There's nothing technically wrong with the man, but he tends to freeze into position like a gargoyle from time to time. I personally think he's just trying not to be noticed by Elvira.

The amazing thing is that those two very different gargoyles managed to produce Annie. Annie isn't mean or petty or cold, she isn't austerely thin or winter white. Annie is a mass of brown curls and freckles and she's not fat by a long shot but she's got curves, which I very much like to get my hands on. I was eyeing them as Annie moved in front of me toward the kitchen, plates in each hand. From behind me Elvira remarked—to whom? I'm not sure who her remarks are meant for, or if they're just general unpleasantries—"In my day, men did not do the clearing of the table, and women knew their place."

I'd gone through the swinging louvered door between dining room and kitchen, and turned back instantly, my mouth open and words starting.

Annie clattered plates to the counter and grabbed my wrist hard. *"Don't."*

I gave her a look, eyebrows up. Because yes, Annie is very familiar with propriety and she knows how to wend her way through a social evening. Thanks to being raised by gargoyles she can converse with the worst and come out of it fine after about fifteen minutes of shuddering and some pillow thumping (we have the most well-thumped sofa cushions ever). But she does know her place. I put her in it not long after we got married six years ago. She opens her mouth when she's told to, bends over when told. She submits beautifully.

It seems to make her stronger. When we got married she was a secretary with a BA in English and the pent-up desire to write. Now she owns a writing agency, hires extra writers, has published several nonfiction books and is either working on a very long and convoluted erotic mystery or is having an affair with somebody at the library where she goes to write on Fridays (that's a joke—it's a novel, not an affair).

Standing in the kitchen, her eyes were full of not panic, but plain fear. Her parents are teetotalers but they're like the alcoholic parents of a friend of mine in college. Elvira picks and picks and picks until someone around her snaps and can't take it anymore and says something, and then Henry rounds off on the offender who dared to question or insult or shut down the wife I'm not sure he notices at any other time. Then there's a screaming fight, because Henry can go from zero to rage like a high-performance asshole.

I really don't understand how those two people produced such a glorious woman.

It's not that Annie's afraid of confrontation, it's that she doesn't see the point, and with the Misery Twins for parents, I can't blame her. Any time someone starts an argument not to win it but simply to have it, they've already won the moment voices are raised.

I swallowed, hard, and followed her back out to the living room with the coffee service.

"Oh, dear," said Elvira. "I thought we were having tea."

Annie started to stand. I sat down next to her on the couch and put one hand on her wrist. "Now," I said, and she subsided. And so that wouldn't sound odd, I said, "Now we're having coffee."

Henry asked me about my business. He always seems offended that my bookstore is still doing well. I think he got a Kindle just to spite me. Elvira asked Annie what she's working on, and Annie told her in breathtakingly dull detail about a series of glossy fliers she was doing for a catering company.

Elvira approves of copywriting work like that. Not too adventurous.

The evening ended eventually. They always do. It only feels as if they don't.

"Now," I said to Annie the minute the door closed behind them. She didn't even glance at the unlocked door or the carelessly drawn curtains over the living room windows. She removed her shirt, her bra and her watch and laid them on the end table beside the door, then knelt at my feet.

"You may," I said, and admired the way the lamplight picked out the gold highlights in her hair and the silver tints on the collar I'd locked around her throat on our honeymoon. She wears charms on it, and polite society pretends it's a necklace.

She paused long enough to give me a dazzling grin that said everything she needed to say about the evening being over, then unzipped my trousers and found me naked under them, rock hard and beaded with want. She pulled my cock out and leaned forward, her tongue out to catch the drops of precome at the head.

"No," I said and put both hands on either side of her head, pulling her roughly to me. Her mouth hollowed, making room in the instant before I slammed into her, fucking her mouth, making her head bob. She made little grunts and moans, her eyes fluttering open and closed, and when she was as deep and as lost as I was, I ordered her to stand, her arms clasped behind her, breasts thrust out at me. I took her strawberry nipples between thumbs and forefingers and began to pinch.

Annie has the most exquisitely sensitive nipples I've ever played with. There are times I've almost made her come by playing with them. When she's on top and I'm slapping them, biting them, pinching them, it all takes her over the edge time after time.

It's always been with a certain amount of control. Little pops. Little scratches. Gentle biting. She can take a spanking, but where her nipples are concerned she's apt to open her eyes wide and suddenly, gasping, start with the word *no* and move on to *red*.

Her safeword. She said it then.

She met my eyes when I looked at her. I hadn't dropped my hands.

"Submit."

Her big brown eyes widened. "Aaron?"

"Submit," I said again.

I saw the conversation come back to her then, one from a couple of weeks earlier, one Saturday morning with no looming parental dinner, when I'd played with her breasts while she was tied to a kitchen chair in the bright sunlit morning. I'd stung them with wooden spoons, dragged the tines of a fork over them and slapped them, and she'd said, "Red," and I'd stopped, but instead of releasing her, I'd pulled a chair up in front of hers, straddled it so I could lay my arms along the top, facing her, hemming her in.

"What do you think about doing away with your safe-word?"

Annie's eyebrows had shot upward; her mouth opened, possibly in protest; and then she'd closed it, slowly, looking confused. "I'm listening," she said, which made me think about that sitcom with the psychiatrist, but she was listening—she was hardly in a position not to—so I talked.

"There's nothing that I'm ever going to do to harm you, or scar you, or do anything permanent we haven't discussed."

When she started to speak again, I urged her not to by the expedience of putting a piece of duct tape across her mouth. This made her grin, because she obviously felt silly or found it funny, which made the tape pull off promptly. Either I have inferior duct tape or those people restrained effectively by it in movies are just wimps. But she stayed quiet.

"We've talked about getting you tattooed," I said. "That's permanent. So is piercing, as long as it doesn't reject." We'd talked about cutting and branding, too, but only in a titillating and horrifying sense.

I reached out and ran one finger down the sweep of her nose, let her briefly suck it into her mouth then continued down the line of throat to breast. Her head tipped back slightly and she let her eyelids flutter. I took her nipple in my fingers and squeezed. Annie groaned and tried to press her hips forward but she was well tied.

I pulled my fingers hard off her nipple and her head snapped forward, eyes opening, mouth starting to form the word *red*.

Only she could take it. I knew she could. I kept my eyes on hers and reached down to stick my middle finger into her cunt.

She was dripping wet.

"Do you trust me?"

"Completely," she said, though her tongue didn't seem to be working quite right, or maybe it was her brain that wasn't working.

"You know I would never hurt you on purpose, and a safe-word can't stop anything that might happen by accident." Otherwise insurance companies would go out of business.

Annie just nodded, staring at me with eyes glazed with lust.

"Think about it," I'd said, and left her there to do so, tied to the kitchen chair.

Most women would sulk at that. Annie had taken her revenge by bouncing up and down on my cock for a very, very long time that afternoon.

I looked into her eyes, and saw that sunny Saturday morning come back. "I submit," she said.

"What is your safeword?"

Her attention had drifted from my eyes, going down my body to focus on my cock.

"Annie. Look at me. What is your safeword?"

"I don't have one," she said. "I don't need one."

In the bedroom I made her finish undressing, then bent her over the bed. She flipped her curls back out of her face and looked back at me. "May I ask what the spanking is for?"

I spank her during sex, when she's over my lap or on my cock, and I love watching her eyes unfocus and her mouth open in pain and pleasure. I love to let my fingers stray and sting her pussy and watch her get on top of the pain, watch the pain turn into pleasure.

When I bend her across the end of the bed, the frame of the four-poster digging into thighs or clit, she's being spanked. Punished. No holds barred.

"I want you to stand up for yourself with Henry and Elvira," I said. "We've talked about this. You said you were unhappy with the relationship. Have you made any changes?"

"No, Sir," she said.

"You use a safeword with them, you know," I said, and when she glanced at me, confused, I said, "'Please.'"

She lifted her chin and nodded.

"I'm the only one I want you to submit to," I said.

Annie let her head sink back to the bed. "Yes, Sir," she said, and I saw her eyes start to close.

I don't know where she goes when she does that, but she wasn't going there now. "Keep your eyes open. I want you present." I didn't tell her to count. She sucks at that, forgetting promptly. So I did, from one to twenty-five, my hand hard and stinging. I crisscrossed her ass, spanking dead center, just under the curve at the tops of her thighs, on her thighs themselves, her pussy. I hit every surface over and over, leaving her red and hot and a little teary-eyed when I told her she could get down on her knees and thank me.

I know some people separate punishment and play, but she takes it well and I enjoy the reward. She sucked hard, and this time I let her do it at her own pace—her head bobbing, tongue working—and when I pulled her up from her knees, I sat down on the edge of the bed and put her on my lap, facing away. She linked her hands together behind her back, clutching her wrists, leaning forward that way, deeply impaled as I started to fuck her. My hands came up and grabbed her breasts, hard, taking fistfuls, grinding them against her chest, pulling my hands off roughly. And then I started on her nipples, slapping hard, harder than ever before; one hand holding her breast, squeezing it taut; the other spanking as hard as I'd spanked her ass, then letting go, letting the blood flow back fast as I grabbed nipples and pinched, hard, hard enough her breath caught; then pulling my fingers off, pinching hard the whole time, pinching, releasing, twisting, using my nails. Hurting her.

I heard her breath catch every time she wanted to utter *red*, every time her mouth automatically started to form the word *no*, every time she stopped herself—and every time she arched against me, head thrown back, cunt dripping around me, sucking hard as she came.

When I came, shooting into her, she gave a little cry and went utterly limp in my arms. I felt a little limp, too, but I'm a gentleman master. I helped her up, tumbled her back down on the bed, followed her down and that was it until Sunday morning woke us.

Another Saturday afternoon and there was a message on the voice mail when we got back to the house. Henry and Elvira didn't seem to hold with cell phones for anything other than emergencies. Actual conversations were held at home, not in post offices and supermarkets. I can't say I totally hate that; not being forced to endure the conversations of complete strangers would be fine with me.

Elvira and Henry also didn't hold with waiting for invitations. The voice mail Annie put on speaker said they would be arriving at 5:30 and would bring a salad, as what Annie had served the previous week had been somewhat tired and perhaps she should consider switching grocery stores.

I puttered in the kitchen, switching on the coffee maker and rummaging for bagels that turned out not to exist. But I was watching my wife.

She didn't know it. She'd gone to that place where she goes when she's working through the outline of a book and trying to figure out why reality is having such a hard time transferring to the written word.

I didn't say anything. I just watched. Watched as she replayed the message, her face going from that faraway working place into sharp reality. She picked up the house phone, dialed, waited, and then said, "Hi, it's me." Pause. Knuckles whitened a bit, fingers clamping the phone. "Well, that's how I say it. Anyway, I wasn't aware we had extended an invitation to dinner for tonight."

Not sure she was going the right way there. I wanted confrontation, not passive aggressive maneuvering.

"I don't believe we did. And tonight won't work for us." Pause. "Because." She floundered. She could say we had plans, of course. But we didn't. Her parents had been preempting our plans for so long that it didn't matter.

Breathe, I thought at her.

"Because we haven't made plans for tonight and weren't planning to have anyone come over."

Okay, I'd set it up. My heart still skipped a beat.

"No, I'm sure you could pick up something on the way, but—" *Breathe*. "That's not the point."

I heard Elvira's voice rise. I heard no words, but I could guess.

"Maybe you should have confirmed with us before three o'clock this afternoon, then," she said. When I looked at her now I didn't have to be covert. Her face was white and her eyes very wide and she had no idea I was there.

On the other end of the phone, the voice got louder and now I could hear the second voice joining in. Henry. I almost said something. My hands locked together as firmly as Annie's when she's told to keep them out of my way.

Annie said into the phone, "Ple—" and I blanched.

And then she stopped. She never finished the word *please*. She stood and listened and I saw reality catch back up with her and saw her lack of interest in what reality had to say. She waited until what seemed to be a very high-pitched squeaking stopped and then she said, "It wasn't my intention to make you feel bad, but it also wasn't my intention for you to assume an open invitation to dinner every Saturday. Let's give it some time, shall we?"

And then my very proper wife breached etiquette and left it trembling behind her in the dust. "Once you and Daddy stop shouting, you can give us a call, invite Aaron and me for dinner, and show me what a proper salad is all about. Or I can pick up a pizza on the way over."

She hung up. Not with dramatic flare, she just pushed off and put the handset back in the cradle.

"How does pizza sound for tonight?" she asked. "With one of those movies where suddenly orphaned children go on to have fabulously happy lives and rule kingdoms?"

I kissed her, swung her around once, endangering kitchen cabinets, and set her back down. "Done," I said. "Pizza. Movie. Beer even. But first, you get a very, very special reward spanking. I need you to take off your shirt. Right. Now."

She didn't even look surprised. She just grinned at me and pulled the T-shirt over her head. "I submit," Annie said.

THE GOLDEN RULER

Giselle Renarde

Hit me, Lowell. Oh, god, I need to feel the sting of your palm on my ass. I need it; I need it; I need it. Are you listening, Lowell? Can you hear me? I need a spanking. Now.

Meghan's face burned as she inched across the carpet. He was sitting on the couch, scotch in hand, acting like she didn't exist. There she was, buck naked, wrists bound behind her back, ankles tied together, and he was pretending she wasn't there. If she had to crawl across the living room like a caterpillar, so be it. Anything to get closer to him.

And he just sat on that leather couch, cool as a cucumber. She wasn't even on his radar, was she?

Look at me, Lowell. I'm down here, laid out at your feet. Can't you see me? Can't you see how much I want you? How much I need you? God, Lowell, just spank me now!

Of course, she couldn't say anything—not with her own cotton panties stuffed in her mouth. Meghan looked up at him pleadingly, but he still wasn't paying attention. He had that jazz station on the radio, and he just sat there with one leg crossed over the other, listening intently. Meghan couldn't see past his knees, but she was pretty sure his eyes were open. His eyes were open, he just wasn't looking at her.

Lowell? Lowell, you know what I need. You're the only man in the world who knows. Why can't you just give it to me? Why can't you look down here at the woman on the carpet and bloody well spank me already?

It was Lowell who'd tied her up this way. She'd knelt on the floor, patient as a saint, naked as a jaybird, and waited with her wrists crossed behind her back.

When she'd entered the room, he was fixing himself a drink behind the bar. The house phone was crooked against his shoulder, and Meghan had jumped when he started talking into it. Because *talking* wasn't at all the right word. *Yelling* wasn't the word, either. It was something in between, a commanding sort of speech, and Meghan realized very quickly who was on the line.

They were having problems with the phone company these days. Meghan usually handled the bills, but she was at her wits' end with this one. Their payments were supposed to have gone down when they bundled their home phone and Internet, but instead they were paying more every month. Each time Meghan contacted the utility, something else got screwed up. Their fees skyrocketed one month, and the next their Internet service was inexplicably cut off.

It was such a huge annoyance Meghan didn't want to think about it anymore. She just wanted everything to be fixed, but she felt like nothing was working. They weren't getting it. They weren't hearing her. All this bureaucratic stupidity was getting her so anxious all her muscles seized every time she thought about it.

"My wife has called you seven times in four months." Lowell's voice was low, and though he sounded entirely calm, it was the kind of tone you couldn't argue with.

Meghan listened keenly as Lowell fed the customer service person all the information she'd muddled through for months. When he took on a task, he made it seem easy. He'd have this resolved in five minutes.

The measured timbre of Lowell's voice had a profound effect on Meghan's body—making her heart race, her pussy pulse, her asscheeks tingle in anticipation. The words didn't matter. This gesture was key. She'd tried and tried to resolve this stupid phone bill thing by herself, but she just couldn't do it. Not alone. And though it had never crossed her mind to ask Lowell for help, it lifted a weight from her shoulders that he'd taken it on.

I'm yours, Lowell. Show me why I'm yours. You can resist me, but can you resist yourself? You know what you want to do. Spank me!

She'd stripped in front of him while he harangued the phone company, and he hadn't batted an eye. He'd watched her intently as she unbuttoned her shirt, opened it wide, slipped it from her shoulders, let it fall to the ground. His gaze burned her collarbone until she'd unclasped her bra and tossed that aside, too.

Meghan loved the way he stared at her breasts—with fire in his eyes, and a snarl in his voice. Any other man would have been rendered mute by the sight of bare breasts, but Lowell went on talking to customer service. His only tell was the growl behind his words. Maybe they took that as a threat. Meghan didn't.

Do you remember that line from A Midsummer Night's Dream? *"Use me but as your spaniel—spurn me, strike me."*

Once she'd stepped out of her skirt and plain panties, Lowell had made his way out from behind the bar. He went off book with the phone company, winging his facts and figures as he bound her wrists and ankles with kneesocks. Even so, the information he conveyed remained surprisingly accurate. One of his most striking qualities was that he actually listened when Meghan spoke.

I am your spaniel, Lowell, right here at your feet. "*The more you beat me, I will fawn on you.*"

He'd bound her and left her on the carpet, returning to the bar where he'd set the stack of phone bills. And his best pen. And his golden ruler. Cork on one side, metal on the other. It wasn't real gold, of course. It looked more like burnished bronze, a business gift, but they'd always called it the golden ruler.

Why won't you look at me, Lowell. I'm right here, down at your feet!

She could hear the woman from the phone company apologizing—a rare achievement in itself—but Lowell didn't say, "That's okay." He didn't say, "No problem." Nothing like that. They gave him what he wanted and he said, "Very good."

Those words ran through Meghan like a storm, making her pussy pulse, clench, want. Ache. Oh, yes, that was the word: she ached for him, and not in any idle sense, not in the sense of juvenile longing. Her pelvis throbbed to be filled by him. If she didn't feel the immense girth of his cock pounding deep inside of her soon, she felt she would really and truly die.

I am yours, Lowell. This body is yours. Take pleasure in it. Use it. Do whatever you want, just touch me with your skin, with your fingers or your cock, or your lips or your tongue. Touch something of you to something of me.

He'd hung up with the phone company and brought his scotch to the sofa, turning up the radio en route. Lowell didn't need to gloat, because she'd heard the resolution through the phone: three months of free service, further reduction in their monthly bill after that, all sorts of perks thrown in. How he managed these things, she'd never know, but every time he took on a task, he battled it into submission. Was there any man more alluring than one who could take on a utility and win?

Please, Lowell. I'm not above begging. You know that about me. I would do anything for you. I'm yours—yours alone and yours completely. You can spurn me if you wish, but I pray you show me mercy. Put me out of my misery, Lowell. Spank me, fuck me, anything!

Once she'd managed her caterpillar crawl across the carpet, the golden ruler became her focus. With her hands tied behind her back, it wasn't easy to lift her head, but somehow she managed, tilting to one side, setting her weight on that shoulder and pressing her forehead up from the carpet. She turned to gaze longingly at the bar. She couldn't speak, could only moan through the damp panties shoved in her mouth, but she slanted her head in its direction and yelped. Lowell knew her well enough to read her thoughts. He'd know. He was sure to know.

The ruler, Lowell. The golden ruler: do unto others...? What would you have me do if our positions were reversed? If it was you here on the floor, your hands tied behind your back, your ankles bound with a kneesock, a pair of dirty underwear in your mouth? All I want is to feel the sweet sting of metal against my ass. Bring that ruler down on me again and again. Smack me, slap me, and don't let up until you've pelted my backside raw. That's what I want, Lowell. I want to be red and ruined. Do it!

How long would she have to wait? This thick tension tied her stomach in knots, but Lowell didn't seem to feel it. Or maybe he just refused to acknowledge it. Maybe he did that to torture her as she crouched at his feet, cheek itching against the rug.

The ruler, Lowell. Spank me with the golden ruler!

He knew. He must know. Why couldn't he get up from the sofa and grab it—it was right there on the bar!

Grab the golden ruler! Smack me with that slip of metal. I want to see it gleam again under soft lights. I want to see it shimmer as you hold it up to strike me, and then hear its length break the sound barrier when you bring it down on my ass. I want to feel that sting.

Do you have any idea how I clench when you punish me? Do you know how much it hurts? It isn't an idle twinge, Lowell. It's pain. It's real pain. Did you know that? Can you hear it in my voice when I scream? Is that why you gag me now? You don't want to hear the anguish in my voice?

He adjusted his position on the sofa, and the leather croaked beneath him.

No, you want it. I know you want it. You take pleasure in my pain. When you spank me with your hand, when you smack me with the golden ruler, when you fuck my throat or ram my ass, you see the tears welling in my eyes. I plead with you. You see the agony on my face. But you don't stop because you know I want more, always more.

And you love me. You give me all this—not only the house and the car and the dealing with the phone company, but the discipline—out of love. I need your firm hand, Lowell. Without your correction, I'd have run off the rails long ago. You keep me in check. You do it for me, don't you, Lowell? You restrain me, you punish me; you make me wait, to teach me, shape me, make me a more resilient person.

The ice clinked in his glass as he shifted on the sofa. When he leaned into its firm embrace she heard him groan. It was a sound of relaxation, pure pleasure. The pleasure of power.

But this is torture, Lowell. To ignore me, to erase me— this is the ultimate wielding of your power over me, over this

woman who loves you more than life. And, Lowell? Lowell?
Can you hear me, Lowell?

And then, with apparent care, Lowell picked his feet up off the ground and brought them to rest in the dip of Meghan's back, nestled right up against her bound hands. The weight of his feet brought out a moan in her, muffled by the panties in her mouth. A connection. Finally, some connection.

I will kneel at your feet forever.

I ALWAYS DO

Kiki DeLovely

My Daddy calls me a word architect. So I pick up my pencil and start drawing up the blueprints to thank him. I make painstakingly precise calculations, planning out every last detail, figuring out how to write him into my life and make the design structurally sound, but it inevitably seems to wobble. Perhaps the most beautiful compositions must.

I've had plenty of Daddies in my day. They've come and gone, dropping in on my life, some having greater impact than others. No matter how many times I've tried to deviate and experiment with other forms of submission, it's always the archetype of Daddy I find myself kneeling at the feet of, time and time again. Daddy/babygirl play just does it for me. It's what gets me going, what gets me off, what gets me there.

This particular Daddy, however, makes me bow my head in an all-new way—I look up at him through thick lashes in awe, batting them just slightly. From the first time I saw him, it was as if he was walking into my life again. He's always felt familiar;

we've had a certain amount of ease and comfort between us. After the first weekend we spent together, I knew this was... different. This was it.

If I hadn't believed in past lives before, his inexplicable presence in my life surely would've sold me on the concept. How could someone—someone who's hardly known me—know me so well? And I him? There's a certain vibration we feel in each other's cells, and the hum of it can be sensed across great distances. It's this unspoken connection that magnifies his dominance over me. And still, amidst the depth between us exists a level of playfulness in the ways we spark off of each other. Before we even got together, he was already my Daddy. And the very first time we played, it started off innocently enough.

"Daddy! Wanna play a game?" I asked sweetly, knowing the answer even before I blurted it out. Yet I waited eagerly for his affirmative response.

"Yes, babygirl, I'd love to."

"Gimme your tongue." And from the moment he stuck it in my mouth, I could feel his hard-on begin to rage. I sucked on it skillfully and diligently, as I would his cock in a few mere hours, but he was only willing to take so much of my game. He wanted to be inside me and he needed it right then.

"Lie down on your back. Spread your legs and close your eyes."

I obeyed. I'm nothing if not obedient. Well, except for the times I'm being bratty...but this was definitely not one of those times.

"Touch yourself for me."

He knew how badly I wanted his cock, so he gave me something else entirely. He wanted to see if I'd acquiesce to what he saw fit to do, to see how far he could push me.

As my fingers tentatively circled my clit, I heard him fumbling around in the nightstand—and was that the sound of latex snapping against skin? The anticipation made me drip. Then I heard nothing. For about five seconds that felt like hours, I heard nothing, but felt his gaze, heavy and proprietary, all over my body. And that just made me all the wetter.

As I started to relax and enjoy the feel of him watching me get myself off, his fingertips brushed my lips apart, the shock of his touch making me jump just a little. His other hand immediately reached for my hip, a comforting reassurance of his presence. I gasped, then sighed and still never once opened my eyes.

His fingers were sliding into my pussy before I caught my next breath and soon he had managed to fit the entirety of his hand inside me. Shifting his other hand from my hip, he pressed the palm of it hard against my belly, as though he was willing it to sink in right through me and meet his fist in my cunt. I writhed under the pressure, reveling in it. Squeezing my eyelids shut tightly so that I wouldn't be tempted to take in his reaction, I felt my muscles spasm one last time as I soaked the sheets underneath me.

"You can open your eyes now, babygirl."

With one hand still inside me, he wrapped the other around my ass and scooped me up onto his lap before I realized what was happening. Breathless and all the more aroused by both the motion and this new, incredibly intimate position, I cooed to him, "You're so strong, Daddy. Not just anyone can pick me up and fling me around like that."

I swear I could see the sparks my eyes were giving off in the reflection in his.

He whispered to me, taking me back down to earth, "I love how I knew the precise moment before you were about to come—just from the feel of your clit getting hard from inside you. I couldn't help but press up against it while you rode your orgasm out against my fist."

That's how he came to have a nice purple bruise on the top of his wrist.

Can't say I had ever bruised someone's wrist before. Or at least not to my knowledge. But his hands are big, like the rest of him. Taller than me, even, and raised in Texas, he's the embodiment of a tall drink of water. I don't remember the last time that I had taken a fist that big...but it had been a while.

A dominant who also just so happens to be a masochist is sometimes hard to find. Don't get me wrong; I'm a bottom through and through. The need to submit runs deep in my veins. But there's coincidentally something so fierce in my desire that it makes me long to dish it out just as hard as I can take it. Luckily for me, this Daddy likes pain. And so I deliver. Sometimes I get to slap him. On special occasions I even make use of a cane or two. And always, always, I bite. Tonight I'm feeling daring. Like pushing the envelope.

"Daddy, may I please..."

He growls in a low voice, "Grab a glove and some lube and work that pretty little hand of yours into my ass, then I want you to bite my nipples until I'm screaming while squeezing my throat with your free hand."

I love his ability to do that—to top me into inflicting pain and give me explicit instructions on how to provide service for him— actions that could, by outsiders, appear as though he's submitting to me, when really it's just the opposite. Profoundly so.

Obediently, I wrap my free hand around his neck while the other slowly opens him up. He groans and strains just slightly against it. This always gets his cock harder than anything else and he starts moving his hand more frantically up and down his shaft, jerking himself off while I work over his ass just so.

It's only a matter of minutes before he's fucking the air, bucking against me. I'm careful to follow his every move while twisting my wrist just slightly, pulling out at exactly the right moment, just as he comes with a series of grunts and tremors, shooting all over my thighs. I chuck my glove into the trash can as he reaches up for me, pulling me into his chest and holding me there. He strokes my hair away from my face, kissing my forehead, my temple, breathing into my ear as he whispers, "Such a good girl," and I almost come. Knowing that I've pleased my Daddy so exquisitely sends me into convulsions, teetering right on that edge. I'm dying to have him repeat it just once more, so his words will thrust that orgasm shuddering through my entire body.

"My good, good girl." And there goes my edge.

My submission begins between my ears, even though it occasionally ends between my thighs. The simplest words of praise given by my Daddy send me soaring. A nicely inserted "Well done" or "Good girl" makes my heart (and cunt) swell with delight. Nothing brings me more pleasure than knowing I've done good by Daddy and have made him happy, hard and proud. In that very second is my life's greatest accomplishment.

I beam back at him as he smiles into me. These are the moments when my submission is the sweetest. The contrast is sharply juxtaposed with the times when he's forcing deep, guttural screams from my throat, though I cherish both equally.

He has this notion that in our past lives together, I buried my texts within him. Never before in his life has he found access to so many words, so he credits me. He says he had safeguarded them deep inside himself for all this time and they're now surfacing by way of his lips, his words and in what I recognize so readily. I pull it out of him; he pushes it into me. The push and pull, the erotically esoteric energy that intermingles between us.

He says he keeps coming back to a particular look I give him sometimes. That look where I'm caught between pain and pleasure, reveling in the simultaneous delight of fear and excitement. Looking like a scared little girl who's about to get exactly what she deserves. I always do.

Later on, he takes me out for dinner and we stop by his office afterward to pick up some files. He does this to me because he knows his work infuriates me—it takes his attention away from me, and the office itself is the epitome of boredom. So I decide to make some fun for myself. I twirl around and plop down on his desk. (He doesn't like when I do things like that—he says it's "unprofessional" and I always mess up his perfectly organized papers.) I wrap my lengthy legs around his spinny chair and wheel him in.

Bending forward so that I almost lose my balance, I interweave my fingers behind his neck and whisper in his ear, "Daddy, you know what I wanna do later on?"

"No, babygirl, what's that?"

"I wanna stick my tongue in your ass."

Flushing about ten shades of pink and red, he's my own personal valentine lit up under my words. He stammers over his tongue then attempts to stutter out a few words, but he can't. Instead he rises abruptly, one of his large hands pushing into my shoulder blades and before I know what's happening, he's got me bent over his desk, my skirt pulled up, exposing my lace panties, and he lands a few really good blows.

Daddy spanks me until I'm crying out and pleading with him to stop, making all kinds of promises I can't keep about how good I'll behave in the future. When he's satisfied that he's pushed me just far enough, he comforts me and wipes my tears away, kissing my forehead, then firmly informs me that I've been much too distracting from his work. Next time I'll have to spend a whole day under his desk, at his feet. And whenever Daddy starts to get too stressed out, he'll put my succulent mouth to work, sucking him off to relieve the tension. I love these types of threats.

As we head back home that night, Daddy turns to me with a wicked look in his eye and says, "Babygirl, you'd better hope that sweet tongue of yours isn't too tired, because you're about to get what you wished for."

I always do.

PINKY

Kissa Starling

P inky twirled her long, pale locks around her index finger as
she read the last page of *Wuthering Heights*. Her American
history book lay unopened on the grass even though she had
a test the next day. Thoughts of Bruce's face flashed through
her mind. His eyes and raised eyebrows signaled anger personi-
fied. *I guess I should have asked permission, but it is my hair.*
Besides, it matches my name. How juvenile was that? She might
as well stick out her tongue and yell "Nana, nana, boo, boo,"
like she did to her father when she was young.

"Exactly the kind of thinking that got you into this mess,
isn't it, babe?" And there he stood. *How in the world does he*
always know what I'm thinking?

"Don't get me wrong. You're more than hot with the pale-
pink curly locks thing going on, but that isn't a decision you
should have made without me. In case you've forgotten, you
shouldn't make any decisions without me." All six foot four of
him towered above her. He pushed a strand of his long black hair

behind his ear, a habit that endeared her to him even more.

"If it weren't for a good cause I would have already tanned your hide good. As it is, your punishment will fit your crime."

How could he say that? He'd yet to tell her what the punishment was. He knew how she hated not knowing. She held back the sarcastic remark that flowed so readily to the tip of her tongue.

Pinky stood, letting the novel fall to the ground. She didn't say a word, but let her gaze wander over his black leather biker boots with the silver chains, which were slightly scuffed and a little more than sexy. Oh, how she'd like to see him use those chains on her.

"Ahh, the silent treatment. You know how I feel about that. I'll get your things. I expect for you to be sitting, back pressed against the sissy bar, by the time I get to the parking lot."

She hesitated for about ten seconds, knowing it would take at least five minutes to get to the parking lot. Bruce didn't admonish her; in fact, he tossed her book straight into her pack, slung it over his shoulder and whistled as he strode away. He rounded the corner of the humanities building and a spark hit her brain like a freight train. *What the hell am I doing? He's going to kick my ass!*

Her legs and feet hustled at the same time and instead of running, she tripped, skinning her exposed knobby knees. Pinky instantly realized her rookie mistake, tears spilling from beneath her eyelids. The challenge was on! Within seconds, she sprang to her feet and ran faster than she ever had. One minute later, the humanities building lay behind her and she could see Bruce's back, twenty feet from the parking lot curb. His incessant whistling seemed to slow down with her approach. Burning air filled her throat. Quitting was not an option.

The choking fit came on without warning. His foot rose to step on the cement. Pinky sped up, stepped onto the curb and sailed into the air, not one ounce of oxygen in her body, landing on the seat of the Road King. She gulped in air, hoping to fill her lungs and face Bruce with an *Aha, I did it* smirk. When she got to the point where she could breathe without wheezing, Pinky looked up. Bruce slammed her bag into her chest just hard enough to knock some of the well-earned air out of her seizing chest cavity.

"I said back pressed against the sissy bar." She scooted her buttcheek back, knowing not to argue. *Dang, how did I forget that part?* Once Bruce sat down and kicked the stand up, Pinky wrapped her arms around him, hugging with all her might. Then she massaged his neck and shoulders while he squealed out of parking lot D and away from Dodd University, where he taught history four days a week. How lucky she'd been when she signed up for his American history class last fall. Too bad she'd had to switch to Dr. Howitser so they could date publicly. Bruce brought history to life.

"Sir, did you see me leap into the air like that?" Pinky smiled, blinking her eyelashes, the wind whipping through her hair. Nothing would hurt her with Bruce as her protector. She saw newly bloomed irises, leaves sprouting and freshly mown lawns, but they all faded away as she focused on her master and what his plan might be.

"I did. Too bad you waited until the last minute to decide my orders were worth following." Bruce sped up, narrowly missing a red light. The rest of their ten-minute ride home passed in silence. He knew how she despised his delayed answers. Game on, indeed.

The brick colonial hovered in front of them. Bruce slammed the kickstand down and removed his helmet. "Clothes off."

Pinky looked toward the neighbor's house.

Bruce grabbed her shoulders, locking his piercing gaze on

hers. "Don't make me ask again. You won't like it."

She pushed her skirt down and ripped off her blouse. Buttons scattered all over the driveway. One hook maneuver and her pink lace bra lay on top of the black leather Harley seat. Pinky flipped her sandals into the air, then knelt before Bruce, head down. *Nothing pleases me more than pleasing you, Sir.*

"So you do remember your place. Follow me, pet."

He'd given no directive to stand so Pinky crawled up the front steps, tiny stones stinging her already scuffed-up knees. She paused, sitting back on her calves, while Bruce unlocked the entrance, smiling and happy to be home. He stepped in and shut the door.

Oh, my god. He's leaving me out here on the front porch? Most of the neighbors came home around six and it had to be after five thirty already. *Thank goodness for these high hedges we planted last year.* She looked to the left and right repeatedly.

The doorknob turned. "Thank you, Sir. I..."

A silver dog bowl, one they'd used many times for their Doberman, clattered against the cement of the porch, spinning, then stilling. "Eat it." Pinky looked to see a mush of brown goo inside. She looked up at her master. *Surely he doesn't want me to eat that.* His stern look didn't change. She shoved her face into the mass of yuck and lapped it up, attempting not to breathe. Ados, their Doberman, ate fast and licked until the bowl gleamed; she knew she'd have to do the same.

Her stomach rolled. *I can't think about it. If I do, I'll throw up and then what? I brought this on myself.* She swallowed without tasting as best she could, slurping the gravy and sitting back on her feet, all in a matter of minutes. Afterward she assumed the position, tongue out and heels digging into her bare, wet pussy.

Bruce reached down and snapped a studded collar around her neck. Pinky thrust her tits out and held her ass high. Her head rose to attention. The leash tugged against her neck; she followed. Ten feet later she crawled through the front door, onto the couch and into her master's lap. "Ass up, babe." She jutted her ass against his waiting hand and wiggled while he rubbed. The first smack came as a slight shock that reverberated through her spine. Her pussy swelled.

Pinky nuzzled against Bruce's arm as he swatted her again, harder this time. His huge hand hit her ass and thighs repeatedly. *Yes, please don't stop.* He pinched her once. "Come." The spasm hit her instantaneously. Like a strung bow, her toes straightened and her head ascended. A tingle fired through her nerves, igniting them into a fiery scream. She didn't know she'd been holding her breath until she collapsed into a heap of useless, spent goo. After-gasms sporadically exploded between her legs.

"You won't make any more independent decisions now, will you?" He formed it as a question, but they both knew it wasn't. Pinky shook her head back and forth.

"I own you, babe. I know what's best for you." She leaned forward, lifting her ass and hoping to guide his hand to land on her pussy. *Please. Let one of those slaps hit my nub.*

"You slut. I'll decide when your kitty gets to join in on the fun." His ministrations increased, going faster and faster. Pinky bucked against his leg. "Always centering your attention on the wrong thing." Her master rubbed his goatee, an evil glint in his eyes.

"Spread your legs and finger yourself. It's time to train the kitty."

She spread wide and pushed her finger into the top of her slit, finding her nub slick with come. Slow circles increased to fast flicks. Pinky's mind whirled with sensations. Round and round, with release so close—imminent. *I love it when he lets me do this.*

"Hands behind your back." The devil voice came from her master's mouth. Reluctantly, she stopped. Her pussy ached and disappointment reigned. Juices trickled down her thighs. Who knew women could have premature ejaculation? Afraid of reprisal, she held back the tears. A scratchy rope circled her hands then bound them together.

"On your knees." Saliva filled her mouth with expectation. Soon he would offer himself to her. Pinky licked her lips, anticipating his warm, hard flesh down her throat.

"Close your eyes."

A soft blindfold enclosed her eyes in a dark oblivion.

Her master's strong hands lowered her down so that the upper half of her body rested against the prickly couch cushion. Pinky's nostrils filled with a pleasantly musky smell. She inhaled, licking her lips once again. An insistent cock rubbed against her ass, exciting but confusing at the same time.

"Lean forward, pet." Doing as she'd been told, Pinky rocked closer to the couch, her nose and mouth making contact with a plump, wet, bare pussy. Startled, she began to pull back but at that same moment her pussy filled with hard cock, which she couldn't help but squirm into. Her position forced her tongue toward the waiting pussy and her nipples against the rough fabric of the couch cushion.

Pinky lapped up the woman's juices, her mouth filling with the divine nectar. The woman moaned then scooted closer. The myriad of sensations merged together. Never before had she experienced such pleasure. Her pussy was full, her mouth was full of pussy and her nipples were being shoved against the coarse-textured couch. Pinky didn't know which feeling to concentrate on. She didn't wish to disappoint either of her lovers.

Her focus settled on her own tits. She aligned her nipples so that they rested upon the cording of the couch cushion. Every time the woman in front of her ground her pussy, it forced her nipples under the cording and every time her master thrust deep into her pussy, her nipples were forced above the cording. The back and forth motion flicked her nipples hard.

One of her lovers stretched her nipple out and attached it to the cushion cording with a clothespin. As soon as it seemed secure the other nipple was attached in the same fashion. Each time Pinky got bounced back and forth, her nipples extended more. Pain seared through her body and pleasure followed right after. She reveled in the ethereal consciousness, giving herself over completely.

Bodies slapped together, one right after the other. The movements quickened. Furious pounding ensued. An explosion of delight expanded to surround every part of her flesh. Come squirted from the pussy she'd sucked and licked. The liquid flowed down her throat as his come filled her own pussy. She'd become a vessel of love; nothing pleased her more. Pinned between two lovers. Every ounce of energy left her body. Behind her, the rope unraveled and cool lotion covered her skin. Some part of her mind acknowledged the light touches that rubbed the lotion on.

Pinky held her breath then came again when the clothespins were removed. The cool lotion pacified some of the burning heat emitting from her previously clamped nipples.

The woman in front of her kissed her forehead, then removed the blindfold, holding her palm against Pinky's eyes. "Open them slowly."

She blinked several times before opening one eye at a time, wanting to speak but not knowing what to say.

Her master took her into his arms, cuddling her naked body close to him. He sat on the couch and pulled an afghan across the front of her. Pinky recognized the soft yarn touching her skin. Andrea sat on the opposite side, shifting close. Together they spoke softly, rubbing her arms and legs. She had no idea what words came out of their mouths, but their tones became the soothing balm she needed. A cocooned feeling of safety and love engulfed her.

"Pinky." The word drew her back to a reality that was more harsh and not so nice as her other world. Her master talked and with every word her mind became more alert.

"I'm okay." She attempted to sit up. Andrea spoke to her, pulling her against her marred chest.

Her master winked her way. "You two catch up." He stood and left the room.

"There, there, little one. You rest. I'm so pleased with you."

"Andrea?"

"Yes, little one. It's me." The older woman stroked her hair as she spoke.

"I dyed my hair for you." Pinky smiled, knowing Andrea would be pleased with that.

"I see. You don't know how much that means to me, little one. I hear your master has something planned for that little rebellion." They laughed together and hugged.

"Whatever the punishment, it was well worth it, Ma'am. Besides, and don't tell Bruce this, but I usually enjoy my punishments."

"You're the first one who's seen me...since the mastectomy."

Andrea, usually such a strong and forceful Mistress, seemed so serious and uncertain with her newly scarred form.

Pinky reached up and traced the scars that made up a newly formed chest. Her lips traced each part of skin the knife had touched.

"Beauty abounds in you, inside and out, Ma'am. It's a pleasure to serve you, as always." Pinky stood up then kneeled before the only woman she'd connected with, on a relationship level. "And if anybody tells you differently, I'll kick their ass."

She smiled as she lowered her head for the ritual pat. "I knew you'd have the right words, little one. At times I wonder who's in charge here, but then I remember."

Andrea smacked the right side of Pinky's thigh playfully. "Get back up here and tell me what's new with you. I've requested a night alone with you and your master agreed. I hope you don't mind."

Pinky hopped on the couch, ready for chatter and fun. She'd missed her friend so much in the last few weeks. "It's his choice, of course, but truth be told, I've begged for time alone with you since the day you went in for surgery. The news of your cancer crushed me. I love you, Ma'am, and I'm so relieved you're okay."

Outside, her master's BMW pulled down the driveway and out into the street. Pinky knew he'd return and that Andrea would take care of her until he did. He'd shared her and taught her to share. That beautiful lesson opened up a whole new side of life that brought her to Andrea and the sapphic love they shared. *It doesn't get much better than this*, she thought. The two women giggled and cuddled. Before the night ended, Andrea would pull in those shared reins, but for now they would share moments and celebrate life.

THE BREAKING POINT

Cole Riley

S ubmission is totally giving up control to another person. That was how the French writer Albert Camus described it. It didn't matter that Camus was talking years ago about the Algerian people being very submissive to the colonist Frenchmen.

When I encountered submission in my life, it was of a different sort. Let me go back to a few weeks ago. After getting off work—as a reporter for a daily newspaper—I went to one of my favorite bars, Costello's, where I saw the mysterious redheaded girl chatting with the bartender. Teddy, the mixologist, was always good for a laugh or two. I sat near the redhead and watched her down shots of bourbon. She was extraordinarily beautiful, with an exotic cocoa face and a body that could bewitch most men and many women.

"I do it because I like it," the girl laughed. "It's not about the money. There's something in my makeup that draws me to it. I still haven't figured it out."

Which were the only words I overheard, but they stuck with

me. She smelled delicious, incredibly enticing. Her aroma filled the space at the bar, a whiff of foreign cigarettes, face powder, rouge and an aura of expensive perfume. It made my heart beat fast.

Two days later, I was standing outside my building in Midtown. I had just been handed an infant by a total stranger who asked me to hold her baby while she tied the laces on a running shoe. I looked up and saw the mysterious girl smiling warmly at me as I readjusted the baby in my arms. The infant wet on me.

"Water sports, huh?" the girl smirked. "What a pretty picture."

I shook my head, replying. "She's not mine. By the way, are you following me?"

The girl laughed gently. She seemed to be eternally happy. Her steps took her away from me to the curb, where she caught a cab. She waved to me from the backseat.

The next time I saw her, it was in the basement of a downtown sex club, and she was hoisted up on this medieval device surrounded by men in suits. Her naked body was trussed up, tied at her waist and at the feet. I was mesmerized by what the men were doing to her; her back was an ugly mess of welts, her buttocks bright red and glowing.

One man reached around her battered body, his fingers going between her legs, dipping inside then lifting them to his mouth to taste her. The other men looked envious.

"I love to discipline young girls," the man said, turning to me. "Are you a member of the club? I don't remember seeing you before."

"A member brought me, I'm just a guest," I answered, watching the others sniff her citrus female scent like randy bloodhounds.

"And who was that?"

"Hugh brought me down," I said, seeing the girl trying to glance over her shoulder at me. She recognized the voice.

"Do you like to be disciplined, slave?" another man, with his tie off, asked her.

"Yes, Sir, I do." The girl stared at her feet.

Without warning, the first man slashed her with a leather whip across the buttocks, not too hard. The girl clearly wanted to yell out, but did not. He leaned toward the girl, stroked her tenderly and put his thick thumb between her pouting, bruised lips. He smiled wickedly at her, reared back and brought the whip down in sharp, stinging strokes. I could tell she loved the pain, the burn and prick of each blow.

"Good girl, slave," he said softly, and kissed her lightly on the cheek.

I walked away through the dimly lit corridors, shaking my head. *How could someone submit herself to that? This shit wasn't normal.*

Later, I saw the girl in the hallway, walking between three men who had just watched her take a beating. They were laughing and joking, teasing her like an unruly lover. One of the fellas even cupped her breast and made a funny face.

Like a fool, I was intrigued by this mysterious girl and waited out front, parked, as the evening went on. Time passed painfully while I kept my vigil. Finally, the men left one by one, getting into taxis or private cars. There was a ten-minute lag before the girl, seeming to relish her time alone, bounced down the stairs, whistling a Katy Perry tune. I was glad I'd waited for her.

I yelled to her and she walked across the street to my car. There was no traffic at this hour. All she wore was a long raincoat and I could tell she was naked underneath.

"Can I come with you, darling?" she asked. "I need to talk. It's been quite an evening."

I opened the car door for her, smiling. Inside the car, the girl sat back and continued to whistle the Katy Perry ditty. She opened the coat slightly, unbuttoning it to reveal the sumptuous curves I'd seen in that small dingy room.

"Why did you go along with the beating from those guys back there?" I asked.

"It's a game." She followed that comment with a chuckle.

I kept my eyes on the road. "Damn, you play rough. Do you like being beaten?"

She giggled. "I like losing control now and then. You should try it. It's being able to go with the flow. Submission means absolute freedom. Most people are afraid to risk that. You see it in their lives; their petty, small lives. It's absolutely freeing to submit to someone."

"I'm too anal," I laughed, slowing down for a red light. "I'm a military brat. Control and conformity are too important for me. My father was an officer in the Army; he stressed rules and regulations during my childhood."

"Oh, boy, what you saw tonight must have rocked your world," she said gleefully.

In my mind, I played a thousand fantasies, scenarios where I was supposed to beat her, spank her or at least make her stand in a corner. At the show earlier, one man had mentioned making her eat out of a dog dish. Another said he got pleasure drawing the words SPERM DUMP on her arching back, leading to her shapely ass.

"I don't understand this," I said. "I don't understand you."

She chuckled again to herself. "Don't be such a wuss."

"I'm not a wuss," I bristled, now looking at her. *Was she so warped as to think this kind of behavior was normal?*

The things I'd seen tonight were way over the top.

She closed her eyes, trying to blot out the world. "Back there, I tried not to move. I didn't want to disappoint the men. The man who beat me would have punished me if I moved."

"Is he your lover? A pimp of sorts?"

"No. Not at all."

"But it hurt...didn't it?"

She let out a long, tired breath. "Hell yeah, it did. My whole body hurt after the working-over they gave me. My legs burned and my bottom throbbed and ached. But I loved it. I loved every minute of it."

"And you didn't blink an eye." I kept looking at her, staring.

For a time, she didn't say a word. Complete silence. Maybe she was thinking about what she had become, a mindless play-toy for these depraved men. I gave her some mental space. I forced my eyes back to the road. She glanced out of the window into the darkness of the night, past the rows of parked cars, the small clusters of people on the streets, the string of lights of the skyscrapers above the intersections.

"You're incredibly beautiful," I said, paying tribute to her unique appearance. So enticing. "Too gorgeous to let those bastards mistreat you."

"So you say. Sometimes beauty can be a liability."

"I don't understand all of this," I repeated.

"And you probably never will. Let me tell you about Sir, the man who beat me. I'm his slave and he's my master. I'm a submissive. I'm capable of doing anything to please him. I give myself to him, going against every rule of society, giving myself to him completely."

"That's crazy. So you anticipate all his desires, all his perversions. From what I saw tonight, he's a big-time freak."

Then a secret smile spread across her face. "Yes, I go deeper into his darkness than he ever imagined. I serve him; only Sir."

"Is this love?"

"No, it's worship for Sir, total admiration and respect. Sir is the only man for me. I could never cheat on or lie to him."

Such a willingness to serve, to submit. Like any man would, I wanted to take her but I knew my dick, the dick of a sane man, would resist. Even the lovely sight of her would not arouse me. I wasn't a pagan. I needed her approval, or even the words and the commands of her keeper, to give me permission.

It was almost as if she was reading my thoughts. "Sir says you'd need to get the green light to fuck me. He knew who you are; Sir knew your soul. Sir knew what you desired, even if you didn't know it yourself. He knew you would be waiting outside after the show. He knew what you wanted."

I turned toward her in disbelief. *I couldn't believe this. How could he know what I would do?*

She put her hand on my leg, dangerously close to my crotch. "Sir says I'm supposed to carry out your every order. Hugh made a deal with him. You know Hugh, right? Well anyway, that's what Sir said. Do you want me gagged, blindfolded or tied up? Do you want me to beg? Do you want your friends to watch or join in? Whatever you want."

I shook my head. "No, no way."

The girl felt between her thighs, slid two fingers inside, and brought them to my mouth. "Can I change your mind?"

She cuddled against me, seducing my willpower. "My pussy's on fire for you. Sir says you will mistreat me just this once. Fuck me senseless. You'll love it. Every moment. Sir says you'll be my master. My god, I want to feel you coming and I want to drink you."

I grinned like an idiot.

"I'll satisfy you, no matter your desire, your pleasure, your fetish. I'll play your game."

I paused. "I feel this is conditional. Did Sir give you to me?"

Her voice grew husky and dark. "Sir says it's a one-time-only thing. You can never see me after this night. Never. No matter how good, how memorable, you can never see me after this."

By the time we got to my place, I was high on anticipation. I couldn't wait to fuck her. She immediately kissed me, her tongue in my mouth, and we blended our bodies as my fingers stroked her soft, smooth flesh. Without words, she kissed me harder, more intensely, and bit and sucked my chest.

I thought about my girlfriend, just fleetingly. She'd like this girl.

Suddenly, in the darkness, the girl seized control. I let her do all the work while she told me to place my hands on the kitchen table. She worked my pants down, underwear as well, and spread my legs, and I sensed her tongue licking me. My legs shook. She ran her tongue along the underside of my dick, causing it to thicken and swell, and she didn't neglect my balls. Her lips engulfed one at a time, until shivers went through my body. When my erection was powerful and throbbing, she swallowed my dick completely in her hot mouth.

"Spread your legs wider, Sir," her voice came up from below. I could feel her circle the head of my sex, flicking her tongue like a cobra, driving me crazy.

When the girl was satisfied with my excitement, she stood up, gripped my shoulders and mounted me. We were glued at the privates, desire and passion surging though our bodies. Her mouth was against my cheek, whispering for me to let her please me, keeping her moves easy and gentle. Her sex was incredibly warm and tight.

"Do you have a breaking point, Sir?" she asked. "A point where the passion rises too much for you to bear?"

"I don't know. I've never been pushed to my limit."

She rode and rode me, writhing with so much force that she was bouncing up and down as if she was being thrown from a bucking mare. Her pussy was very wet. Her fingers worked at her clit, keeping pace in the frenzied rhythm we had set. Our eyes met.

"Fuck me, Daddy, fuck me as hard as you can," she panted. "Use me like the filthy slut that I am. That's it, that's it. Rub the head of your dick against my clit—oh, damn, oh, damn—before you shove it back in me. I love it when you pound me hard like that. That's it. Stretch my hole with each thrust. Please, please, please fuck me...."

I began to fuck her roughly, trying to drive my hard pole into the bottom of her sex. She loved it. She said she needed it. She told me I had the thickest, biggest dick that ever fucked her. I knew it wasn't true, but it sounded good.

"Will you stretch my pussy for me, will you stretch my asshole for me?" she whined. "I want you to pull my hair while you ram it in. Will you fuck my tight ass, pound it until it is raw, open and oozing?"

Crazed with desire, I reached up, pinching her thumb-sized nipples as I thrust mightily into her. She was coming while I pinched them hard. I pulled her hair as hard as I could. Another squirt of hot fluid flowed over my dick before a wave of lust snatched my breath away. I kept coming into her and then she dropped down and covered my spurting dick with her mouth, squeezing my balls, and it seemed to go on a long time. I yanked her up and she told me to slap her hard. I did as I was told. She didn't even cringe. One of my hands found her clit, stroking slowly and in a steady circular motion. That kept her twitching with the pulsing of another orgasm already upon her. She let out a long shriek, and I pulled her to me. I put myself back into her, her muscles tightening around my hard flesh, and stayed inside her for quite a while afterward.

"I can see why Sir said I can only do you once," the girl said. "You're a dangerous man, quite dangerous." She cut on the light and went to the bathroom. I saw the ugly welts.

I followed her, sat on the toilet and smoked a cigarette.

"What are you, sweetie?" I asked. "That's right, no questions."

She winked. "I'm complicated." She hopped into the shower and I gave her a towel.

"It's a shame you're taken," I said between puffs, and she smiled wickedly.

SHINING IN
THE DARK

Bex vanKoot

S he laid the wide canvas out onto the floor of the small play
space very carefully, her freshly scrubbed feet tiptoeing
daintily from one corner to the next; she tacked it down all
along the floorboards, leaving only a small track between the
edge and the wall for a safe entry and exit. Her deft moves
made it clear how many times she had done this before, and just
thinking about all those incredible sessions started Adam's cock
stiffening, pushing to free itself from the long, thin robe as he
watched her from the hallway.

She moved in silence, gorgeous and graceful as always, even
with her ankles hobbled by the rope cuffs that forced her to
take tiny careful steps, naked but for the thick leather panties
that locked tight at her hips. Light, nervous chitchat filtered in
from the living room where the other four contributing artists
sat in matching robes and waited to be invited into the studio.
It had been months of planning, testing and boundary setting
to bring this all together, and weeks of hard work. Tonight

would be their final night together and everyone was on edge.

Adam stood back and admired their work thus far. Last month, Lily had gone through the same painstaking routine with this same canvas and after she had taken her place, laid out like a gorgeous star in the center, they had gone to work painting her beautiful body. The men had taken turns with their paint and his wife in the center of the room while the rest watched, masturbated and made colorful messes of their own bodies in preparation. Yellow, red, black and blue paints were rubbed, brushed and caressed into her skin and when she was covered in color, when each corner of the canvas was painted in one hue of handprints and footprints and butt prints from one of the four men, they had finished her off with a film of hot come and left her there to dry. Adam had waited until she was able to stand again and carried her very carefully through the maze of wet paint to the shower so she could rinse off, leaving a gorgeous white void behind like a blazing shadow.

After he had gently washed her and rubbed her skin with a soft towel, he had given her the good news. The look on her face had been priceless.

"A whole month?" she had asked with that tragically beautiful edge of self-doubt.

He had smiled at her, taken her cheek in his hand and kissed her lips. "Yes. Will you sacrifice your orgasms for an entire month? Can you do that for me? For your art?"

She didn't take the question lightly. He remembered getting hard just watching her think about it, commit to doing it even though she knew it would be excruciating. She also knew it would be exquisite. She had nodded, but he wanted to hear her say yes. This would be the longest she had gone without an orgasm since her husband had bought her that very first vibrator, the beautiful toy that finally made her come for the first time when she had opened herself up to him nearly four years ago, before their wedding, before she had agreed to become his and before he had given her everything—the gallery and the inspiration to fill it. He had introduced her to this side of his sexuality, the pain and domination she had always craved but never known, with the same slow unbearable patience he took every time he gave her pleasure or pain.

"Yes, Sir. I promise that I will not come until we finish this canvas."

Satisfied, he had lain back and watched her tortured eyes well up with hot, wet excitement and tears to match the hot, red wetness in her cunt as she sucked his cock with the perfect skill that belied her years of training. They both knew this would be her greatest challenge yet.

The next night he had brought home the chastity belt. She had whimpered just slightly when he locked it into place. Except to shower, during which time she was closely monitored, she had not been allowed to take it off. It looked gorgeous on her and Adam could tell by the slick look of her thighs that even the tight leather couldn't hold her wetness in. She was dripping.

When she had finished prepping the room, she walked to the center of the canvas and stood, staring at him in silence. Her usual silly smile was shadowed by a solemn and furrowed brow and he knew it was time to get started, before her worries got the best of her. He took off his robe and picked up his toolbox, calling to the men in the other room: "It's time."

Surrounded by the four naked men for the third time in her life—there had been a larger group for their auditions—she closed her eyes and let their smells and the sounds of them moving bring her back to her last orgasm. The memory revealed itself between her legs, her hips gently swaying from side to side so that her sex splayed unconsciously outward toward an eager crowd, even hidden inside the leather case. Adam approached her slowly, meeting her gorgeous face with a wide grin. She smiled back now with her usual confidence. The smell of his sweat and the brush of his hand to sweep her hair from her eyes were all she needed to know she was ready.

He moved behind her at a snail's pace, savoring every second of the slow expansion of pleasure and awareness she experienced as their breathing began to sync and her mind began to sink deep into that place where the magic happens. She closed her eyes and he slid the blindfold into place, dropping her into darkness. He inserted an earplug into each of her ears and pulled her hair back into a loose ponytail.

Adam untied the ropes that attached her ankle cuffs and stood up, taking the key from around his neck. Though he could have easily worn the chastity key himself, he had wanted Lily to be always reminded of her wanting. He unlocked the back of the gorgeous platinum collar he had given her on their wedding day. From it he slipped the key to her belt and locked the collar quickly back in place, holding her neck and jaw in his strong hands for just a moment. The pressure took her breath away and she shivered with excitement.

He didn't hesitate removing the belt, unlocking each tiny metal latch quickly and pulling the leather to the floor. The scent of her excitement filled the room and she shivered again with her hot skin exposed to the cool air. He pushed her legs roughly apart and grabbed the spreader bar from the rack hanging on the wall at the edge of the small room. With her body sufficiently accessible, he tied a cuff on each wrist and one by one, the men who stood just off the canvas in the corners of the room came to him with the ropes that were anchored at the floor and ceiling of each of the four points. He latched the metal clips in place so she was suspended with her legs held in

place and her arms immobilized out at her sides, once again a
star with the white space of her body filling her shadow on the
canvas below.

Adam stood back to admire his work. He touched her breasts
and let his hand trail down her abdomen and hip, finding her
inner thigh. She sighed. He got close enough that she could
hear him in her dark, quiet void. "You are a star shining in the
dark."

The energy in the room grew thick as the men gazed at her
naked body, their own arousal growing as Adam left her side
to grab his implements. When he was ready, he put one hand
around her neck and the other on her back, pushing her forward
so she was bent at the waist with her arms out like the wings of
a proud bird—time to fly.

He smacked her ass hard, without any warning, a bare open
palm that left a large red welt. She cried out and he rubbed the
hot spot. He needed to hurt her first. She needed paint for her
canvas. There was going to be blood. Despite the growing lump
in her throat, her cunt fluttered with excitement. Adam beck-
oned to the man in the first corner and his cock jumped to life
as he approached the young woman in the center of the room.
He took her by the shoulders to support her, his cock bouncing
up and down in her face, and she opened her mouth wide and
Adam stroked her hair, acknowledging her obedience. The hard
flesh in her face found her waiting lips and plunged into the
back of her throat, pulling out after only a few quick strokes.

Lily knew why when the cane came crashing down onto her
exposed backside, painting its screaming pain in one thick red
welt across her skin that sang hot praises to Adam's strength
and skill. She sang with them, her voice rising and falling in a
long wail that was cut short by the hard cock once again seeking
out the depths of her mouth. The man would prod at her gag

reflex just until her breath began to run out, then Adam would wind up and land the searing pain upon her flesh once, sometimes twice until she was a screaming, sobbing mess. Somewhere just on the edge of too much, as the welts began to melt into one another and she didn't think she could stand it any longer, the edges of her body began to blur. When the first blow broke through her delicate skin and the blood began to flow, she was gone and her spirit soared outward, filling the entire room. Adam didn't stop beating her and as her body relaxed into the pain, her jaw went slack and the cock on her tongue broke past the tight walls of her throat. The man moaned as she swallowed him, nodding to Adam that he was close.

With tiny rivulets of red running down her ass and her thighs, the first ribbons of semen splashed over her skin, making beautiful patterns in the sweat and blood and bringing her back to the stinging pain. Spent, he retreated back to his corner of the room and sat down on the wood floor, waiting and watching. Adam moved to flank her left side and took a breast in one hand, lifted her up slightly so he had better access to her soft flesh and a view of her pretty lipstick-smeared face. The next man moved quickly and grabbed her by her hips, guiding her onto his solid dick in one smooth movement. She cried out as her battered and quickly bruising body bumped up against his, but he didn't hesitate, pulling out and diving in again, then again, the sounds of her pleasure and pain driving him forward. He fucked her hard and fast and Adam could tell she was close to coming. He got in close again and made his voice loud and stern. "Not yet."

The second man finished quickly inside her, fucking furiously in uncontrolled motions that forced Adam to steady her body to keep her from falling. He walked away and left her breathless with hot come dripping down her legs. She jumped when the third pair of hands grabbed her by the hips but only dipped a hand into her sex, rubbing the hot mixture of juices on himself before spreading her swollen ass wide and probing her little star with his finger.

When she backed her hips up toward his eager hands, he positioned himself carefully and slowly pushed his way in past one and then two tight sphincters, holding himself there gripped tightly inside her. As they stood there motionless, Adam slid the needle into her flesh, the pin pointing precariously at her nipple so that even the slightest sway would prick her. The blood trickled along the cold metallic shaft in her breast and hovered there, clinging to the tight bud at the peak. One more thrust from the man buried in her sacrum sent the drop flying onto the canvas, and then another needle joined the first. Another short burst of hard thrusts followed by a needle, then another and another until they radiated out from the center in a shining silver star. The man behind her moved faster and faster each time, his hands digging into her flesh where Adam had marked her.

The thrusting in her ass grew insistent and Adam moved to the other side, inserting a new needle whenever the man got close and slowed his pace. He moved his hands from her bloody ass to her shoulders, smearing red across her back as he made his final thrusts, bucking wildly as Adam held her in place with his eyes fixated on the tiny red droplets that fell from one breast, then the other. The man behind her let out a loud yelp and unloaded his climax inside of her. When he pulled out, Adam quickly undid the ropes that held her hands and arms in place, and the fourth man joined him to help lay her down on her back, blood, sweat and come seeping from her broken body and soaking the canvas.

The last man quickly climbed onto her chest and, grabbing her swollen, bloody breasts, slid his cock between them and pressed them tight. Adam removed her blindfold and stood back at her feet, stroking his cock as she looked at him with pleading eyes and whimpered through the pain. Tears finally sprung from those deep blue wells and the salt and sweat smeared mascara and sent it trailing down her cheeks. "Please." Only one word, but it caught Adam off guard. She was usually silent and wordless during their scenes. The man above her watched her tortured face with delight as he continued to plunged into her ample cleavage. "You want my come? You need it, don't you?"

She nodded, no longer focused on Adam but the man whose cock nudged at her chin. Adam would have made her say it out loud, forced her to admit her cock-hungry come-loving ways, but the other man didn't need to hear the words. Just knowing it was true sent him tumbling over the edge, splattering her face and chest with hot, sticky streams of his delight.

Adam finally approached her. As the man collapsed in his corner, Adam knelt by her side and slowly removed each of the needles, leaving a pattern of bloody pinpricks in circles around each nipple. She smiled at him and he gave her a quick nod before flipping her around on her belly, the mess on her chest and her face another layer on the canvas.

He knelt between her legs and entered her slowly, leaning forward to pin her arms to the ground. He removed the earplug from one side and whispered, "Are you ready to shine?" He began moving rhythmically, slowly at first but then finding a steady pace. "Can you feel it, Lily? Weeks now without an orgasm, can you feel it? Do you want it? Where is it?" She let out a loud moan.

"Not good enough, lover. I want you to tell us all how badly you need it. How much does this art mean to you? What does it make you feel?"

She let out a deep sigh. Her voice quivered. "I want to come. I want to come forever."

He didn't stop fucking her, continuing to move at just the right pace to keep her on edge. "I want you to come, too. Do you know why I want you to come?"

She was silent, thinking.

"I want you to come for me, because you are my shining star. You shine for me. I give you the darkness, and you give me the light. You can burn so bright that long after you're gone, you will still shine all across the universe. Do you understand?"

She tried to nod with her face plastered against the floor. "I'm yours. My orgasm is yours." She smiled. "I want you to have it. Please, let me give my orgasm to you. Let me shine."

He kissed her forehead and whispered, "You belong to me because you belong to the world." She closed her eyes and he picked up his pace, finding the perfect angle and fucking her with abandon as her body began to tense and twist beneath him. She let out deep sobs of pleasure and pain as it welled up in her, came crashing down again and overcame her. Through her broken skin the light grew, through her moans the light shone and as he came to a violent finish, pummeling her body with his own, she exploded into a shower of light, scattered over the canvas like fireworks.

ROOM #3

Emily Bingham

The door is barely open a couple of inches before a strong arm is grabbing my wrist to pull me into the room. His fingers grip with a firmness that means I can't pull away as he twists it behind me and into the small of my back. Using this leverage on my wrist, he pushes me against the wall hard enough to knock the air out of me as he kicks the door closed with a sinister slam.

He locks it, the finality of the clicking of that bolt echoing in the room and my head, a reminder that the time to turn back has come and gone. The moment I knocked on this door, I consented to become his plaything. From here on out I have no say in what will happen. No words are to leave my mouth in this space; I am at his mercy. I can only hope I've made a wise choice.

My body is pressed against the cold wall, him leaning into my back, wrenching my wrist at intervals to elicit small pained gasps. Already I'm panting, which makes him chuckle sadistically in my ear. All I can hear is my heart racing and his breath against my neck. He spends what feels like forever enjoying this moment, allowing my adrenaline to build.

I move my head a bit to the side in order to see him. This is a mistake. He grabs my hair with his free hand, the one that until now had been resting tenderly against my waist. My head is pulled at a sharp angle so that all I can see is ceiling. Each breath is a struggle with my head tipped this far back, but at least he has unpinned me from the wall.

With my unbound hand, I ineffectually claw at the fingers in my hair until he takes that limb out of the equation by grasping both my hands in his, now trapped between our bodies and twisted between my shoulder blades. His other hand is on my neck now, a soft lover's caress, all tenderness and reassurance, a messy contrast to the pain in my shoulders. Even I know what comes next, that he's messing with my mind, letting me get comfortable before his next move.

Though I'm prepared for the moment his grip on my neck becomes tighter, the suddenness still takes me by surprise. He cradles my head into the crook of his shoulder while very literally holding my breath in his hand. The pressure on my throat means if I hold very still I can get enough air to stay conscious but also requires me to fight the very strong urge to not panic.

He makes small soothing noises in my ear while tightening his handhold little by little. My knees are starting to melt, my body is begging for just one big gasp of air, a gift he isn't prepared to let me have. Soon I'm falling against him, unable to hold myself up. He catches the weight of both of us and begins to move me toward the bed.

Dragging my near-limp body across the room is no effort at all for him. He's apparently much stronger than I had thought. This realization somehow sparks the first genuine bit of fear in me. I begin to struggle as best I can in my breathless state. This gets me nowhere and wastes the last reserves of air I had left. He chuckles again at my predicament.

Just before being tossed facedown on the bed, I catch sight of the armchair in the corner. There is someone in it! Another bout of dread passes through me, and I try once again to get away. We were supposed to be alone; there was no mention of a second man!

I recognize the person sitting comfortably and smiling at the show as my face is shoved into the scratchy comforter. It's the man who should have me in his hands. The man I had planned all this wickedness with. If he's watching from afar, who is holding me down on the bed?

My arms are quickly shackled behind me, and a gag placed in my mouth. I can't get free, and I can't call for help. My heart races as the mystery man takes his hands off my bound body and walks away.

"Quite the situation you've gotten yourself into." The sound of my friend's voice causes me to go stiff. Both of my captors snicker. Someone grabs my hair and pulls my head off of the bed and begins caressing my face, saying, "Aww...poor thing."

Four hands lift and place me in the center of the bed. "Shh. No need to struggle, sweetness, it won't do you any good. We have big plans for you no matter how much you fight it."

He presses my face into the blankets. The other person in the room walks around the bed and I feel his weight on the other side of me on the mattress. Something goes warm and electric at the center of me; I can't tell whether it's panic or arousal but I stop fighting and go limp as it runs through me.

Someone tips me onto my side so I can look into a familiar face. Only the intensity in his eyes and a firmness around his jaw betray some of the thoughts dancing in his mind. He takes my chin in his hand and tips my head toward him.

"Look at me. I said, look…at…me." The edge in his voice causes me to comply. For a long and loaded moment, we lock eyes, his hard and mine pleading. "Be brave. You'll be okay, sweetness."

He gives a nod of assent to the person behind me. The last thing I see is him standing above me before a blindfold is cinched tight. My remaining senses are in a frenzy and I struggle to hear where my captors are in the room, to anticipate their next move. Someone turns on music just loud enough to muffle their movements, and suddenly I am totally lost.

I wait.

When someone finally sits down on the bed in front of me and begins to unbutton my shirt, the physical contact is actually a relief. Soon this turns into my nipples being twisted and pulled harshly. At this point all I can do is whimper through the gag. The other set of hands in the room push my skirt up and begin fondling my ass, grabbing and smacking it at intervals.

"Mmm, no panties. Good girl, following orders so well." It's my friend's voice again; the mystery man remains disturbingly quiet. "Should we reward her with a good fucking?"

The fondling becomes rougher and more sexually charged. I'm tossed on the bed between two much stronger bodies that make no secret about their enjoyment of treating me like a rag doll. Fingers enter me roughly. A tongue is run around my lips where they are spread over the ball gag. Hands alternately pet and pinch my breasts. A cock is pressed against my belly. Teeth nip at my neck, thighs, nipples.

A surrealistic parade of body parts brush against and have their way with my naked and defenseless skin. Throughout this manhandling I have no way of knowing who is doing what or what will come next. However, even blindfolded and in a frenzy of lust, the sound of pants being unzipped and dropped to the floor is unmistakable. All of the air is forced out of the room by that small sound. It is so silent suddenly it seems no one even dares to breathe. I know for certain what series of events will now unfold.

One of them grips me from behind and pulls me to his chest as he sits on the bed against the headboard, my hands now pressed to his crotch and held there between our bodies. His cock is hard in my hands. I stroke it. He uses my hair as a handle to hold me firmly against him as the weight of the other man joins us on the bed, moving in between my legs. This man ratchets my thighs wide apart, clawing at them as he makes his way into position to have his way with me. Held against the first body, there is no room for me to wiggle away as he enters me.

With a cock in my bound hands and another deep inside of me, all I can do is moan and lean into this warm body. I can feel his breath on my face as he holds my hair, while his counterpart literally fucks me silly. After a couple of minutes of being trapped between these men, I lose myself to the experience, moaning and enjoying the rhythm of their thrusts.

Just seconds before I feel myself about to come, he must decide that I am enjoying myself too much. Suddenly everything stops and I groan sadly, bucking my hips as best I can to hope to convince whoever was fucking me to continue. I hear a sadistic laugh, then hands working at the buckle on the blindfold.

"Don't you want to know who is working you over before we continue, sweetness?"

Now I know my friend is the body behind me. As the blindfold falls, the other man resumes his perfectly timed hip movements. I blink my vision back into functionality, adjusting to the light of the room. Once again I feel on the verge of orgasm, having a hard time deciding whether to open my eyes or close them in pleasure. He speeds up to force me over the edge as I finally get my first glimpse of his face.

In the throes of a warm, body-shaking orgasm, it takes me longer than it should to place this man's face. He seems awfully familiar but out of context and with my brain scrambled I can't figure out who he is. As I rattle my mind for any clue, he continues the relentless pounding of his hips against mine, working his way deeper inside me with each thrust. As my legs wrapped around him draw him in, he finds the perfect rhythm to drive me absolutely mad. I can't stop coming over and over again until I'm quivering between them, one man inside me as I hold the cock of the other in my hands.

My uncontrollable orgasms eventually drive the stranger over the edge as well. He smiles in the midst of this, and suddenly I know exactly who he is.

Three-shot Americano, no room for cream, in a twelve-ounce to-go cup. Every weekday afternoon at about two he comes in, perfectly coiffed and wearing a dark cut-to-fit suit that hugs his every curve. Every girl with a functioning libido at the upscale coffee shop I work at has a raging crush on this man, me included. And with good reason—not only is he hot as hell, he's sweet, smart and tips well. Then there's that impish smile!

Since he had become a regular, I'd had a number of toe-curling masturbatory fantasies about this man tossing me over the closest piece of furniture. The fact that he was actually here in bed with me at this very moment made me briefly question my sanity.

"You can't say I never got you anything good, sweetness. Do you like your present?" I nod. My friend cooing in my ear lets me know this is actually happening, and now I'm so impressed with his planning it makes me dizzy.

As Mr. Americano is busy recovering from his exertions, my

friend crawls out from behind me and lets me drop back on the bed. They grin at each other, far too pleased with themselves. As if in answer to the confused look I direct at him, Mr. Americano gives me a playful *aw shucks* shoulder shrug and says, "What can I say, darling, couldn't resist the chance to have at it with my favorite coffee gal." And there was that slight Southern twang to his voice, making me melt all over again.

While I'm distracted, one of them rolls me facedown on the bed. The cuffs and gag are removed. I flex my fingers and jaw, enjoying the freedom that I'm sure won't last long. My head is forced into the mattress, a reminder of my place in the scheme of things even though I'm no longer bound. One of the men guides my hands into the small of my back and holds them there. I can feel his naked body rubbing against my ass, teasing me while holding me down. Raising myself off the bed, I arch toward him like an animal in heat, feeling just the tip of his hardness touching my thighs. I sigh, desperately wishing I could ask for more attention.

A chuckle in front of me and then I hear in that sexy drawl, "You weren't kidding—she *is* quite the insatiable little slut." He pulls me by the hair, raising my head off the bed and guiding my face into an angle where I make eye contact with him. He looms over me.

His cock is now at face level and I can't help but admire it, hard once again, thick and just the right length, much like I had dreamed about in all those fantasies. And now here he is actually directing it into my mouth. I gladly accept it, drawing it into my throat as far as I can, which apparently isn't far enough. He uses the handle of my hair to control the speed at which his cock violates my mouth, making me choke, gag and drool all over him in that humiliating way he appears to enjoy so much.

This show seems to inspire my friend as I feel him enter me

from behind. Now I'm being rocked back and forth between two cocks, being taken from each direction, lost in this blissful lusty oblivion where I have no say in what happens to me. My body is nothing but a toy for their pleasure. Occasionally I look up to see Mr. Americano lost in his own elation, his hands wrapped in my hair, grinning evilly.

When they tire of their current position they switch, my friend throat-fucking me and the dreamy, still-nameless customer pressing himself into my pussy. "Look at me, don't you fucking dare look away," insists my friend. It's harder than one would think to maintain eye contact with someone as he has his way with your face, especially while choking on his cock. This also makes it impossible to drift away to my happy place. Instead I am fully aware of every moment of being used, which I suppose is part of the fun for him.

I watch as he works himself into a frenzy, ultimately coming in my mouth, holding his cock in my throat so I have to work to swallow around it, not wanting to spill any of him on the bed. After removing himself from my mouth, he laboriously wipes his cock off on my face, using one hand to steady my head so I can't turn away. The other he uses to hold his cock as he dries it on my cheeks, forehead, neck. When he's finished, I'm a mess and still being hammered into from behind. Soon I feel Mr. Americano pull himself out, remove the condom he's been wearing and come all over my back, marking his territory with a grunt.

They leave me panting, sweaty and come-covered on the bed, allowing me to catch my breath for a few moments before one of them returns. Mr. Americano gently moves my arms to my sides and massages life back into them after having pinned them down against my back through much of this ordeal. I am exhausted but beginning to feel human again as he touches me compassionately.

I come out of my euphoric state when I feel him flipping me over onto my back. He then takes my hand and guides me up off of the bed and into the bright opulent bathroom. Still clasping my hand, he helps me into the shower with him, turning on perfectly body-temperature water that engulfs us. We are silent as he soaps up my body under the spray, being very thorough and attentive. When he reaches between my legs, he becomes even more focused.

He guides me against the wall of the shower so I have something to lean into as he rubs my clit, which is desperate for attention after being ignored while the rest of my body is worked over. It doesn't take long, between his fingers massaging my G-spot and my clit, for me to come again. For the first time all day, I have my hands free. It takes me a while to realize I can use them to hold on to the beautiful body of this man in front of me. So I do, grasping at his hips, fondling his chest and soft cock as he forces me over the edge a few more times in the slippery tub.

If I had more energy, I would try to elicit more from him. Though it's plenty interesting in its soft state, his cock is even more fun when hard. I sigh as I run my hands over him a few more times before returning the favor and soaping him up, enjoying running the bubbly bar of soap over every curve of him. It's like seeing his body for the first time now that I'm unrestrained and able to experience it for myself.

When we're finished rinsing ourselves, Mr. Americano turns the water off, gives me the signal to stay where I am and steps out into the bathroom to get a towel. He brusquely dries his own body as I watch, before bringing a towel over to me where I stand dripping into the tub. He then dries me off gently. I feel very pampered by the time he's done, especially after the roughness of the rest of our time together.

He reaches out his hand for me, helping me step out of the

tub so he can wrap the towel around my body long enough to take me back to the bed. Lifting the covers, he guides me under them to tuck me in. I smile sleepily at him as he says thank you and good-bye to my friend, the two of them grinning like madmen, thrilled to have pulled this encounter off. He circles around the bed to sit on the edge I'm facing.

"Good-bye, darling. Thank you for the lovely afternoon." He kisses me on the forehead while I lie curled up under the covers of the big posh bed. "Remember, as far as your fellow coffee maidens go, this never happened. If you can keep our secret, I'll see you every day at two for the best cup in town. If you're a really good girl, I'll even ask for another round one day. Understand?" He takes my chin gently in his hand and winks.

I nod and smile at him as he walks out the door. It's a shame to see him go but I'm glad the afternoon's festivities have come to an end; I can't handle any more manhandling right now. As soon as the door clicks shut, my friend crawls in the bed with me. He curls into the curve of my back and holds me against him, entwining me tenderly and tightly in his arms, a pleasant end to our time together, some sweetness after all the struggle.

Back in coffee land, Mr. Americano makes good on his word. I continue to see him every day over the chrome and wood divide of the high customer-service counter, doing my best to not let on that we ever crossed the customer/barista line. Luckily, all of us who work in this café have such a crush on him, it isn't that unusual or noteworthy that every time he walks in I flush bright red as I remember our time in that hotel room together. My mind flashes back to the debauchery while trying to pretend he's just another customer.

Always a gentlemen, he gives me a little knowing wink whenever it happens while I take his order. Other than that, seemingly nothing has changed between us. I keep waiting for the day he slips me a note, or I get a call to meet him somewhere. Maybe it will never happen, but it gives me something to look forward to and keeps me on my toes each time my friend calls. I never know when I'll end up in another room trapped with the two of them again.

The thought makes me wet.

DUO

J. Sinclaire

There is a delicate balance to submission, whether it is physical or emotional, that is part intuition and part (oh, the perverse irony of it) faith. Not existential, "this is simply not enough" faith, but the willful belief in something or someone that allows us to completely let go. To not be caught up in the self-conscious pretense of day-to-day work and life and cubicles. To not be concerned with ourselves beyond the flush on our cheeks and the cock between our lips. To just let go of anything that could in any way prevent this—this release. This roiling storm of ecstasy. This orgasm that shatters our bodies, again and again, until we are weak and spent, and can fuck no more. This, at any sane cost.

Submission is the first step on a path fraught with pleasure.

I suppose that's why I'm here. Here being standing between two handsome men who are more than willing to assist me with any desire I could conceive of, or even concoct a few new ones if need be.

We're somewhere private enough, with seating nearby and a counter behind us. They are stocky, solid and strong, similar but all part of a delightful combination when submission comes into play. We are at that moment when intent becomes action, and my heart is already racing.

James makes the first move. Bridging the gap between us in a single step, his hand snakes around my waist and draws our bodies close. Though only slightly taller than me, it is enough that he has to lower his lips to meet mine and he does so slowly, allowing us a few shared breaths first. The anticipation swells, and the eventual kiss makes my cunt ache with demands for attention.

We are frenzied. I tease him with my tongue. He nips at my lip. His fingers dig into the curve of my hip and I can feel his cock stirring against me. My arms lift to drape around his neck and we both lean into each other instinctively. A murmur of pleasure passes my lips, unbidden, as he coils his hand into my hair and tugs sharply.

Our lips part, my head is thrown back, and his tongue and teeth graze along my jawline to my neck.

"What do you want?" he questions me, blunt and demanding.

My scalp stings but my pulse quickens as I compose my reply. "What you want. Fuck me. Use me." My voice trembles at the thought and my pussy responds wetly to the image. "Both of you, everywhere. Just make me come harder than I ever have."

Hal chuckles behind me, amused in part by my words and by James's subtly shocked reaction. His cursory surprise does not escape me either; I can hear his breath stutter, a momentary pause in the rhythm, as my statement sinks in.

Hal is well aware of my proclivities, my brash statements and my imploring pleas, but James...James is about to learn.

As am I, I realize, when James shifts his other hand from my hip up to my neck. He cups me under my jaw, thumb and forefinger holding me in place firmly. A smile flickers across my lips, a thrill I can't hide, enjoying his immediate response to my request.

His words, like his lips, are soft and moist against my ear. "You're damn right you'll come." I murmur nonsense in agreement.

"When I want you to."

He punctuates his statement by shoving me down onto my knees in front of him. Eye level with his cock, I watch as he frees it from his pants. He is hard, thick and weighty, precome glistening on the tip of his head. I moisten my lips with my tongue, eager to taste him.

One hand tangled in my hair, the other stroking himself slowly, James pulls me close enough that I'm able to lick a trail along the underside of his cock. He shifts his body slightly, letting go of my hair to reach behind him, gripping the countertop to steel himself.

Able to move more freely now, my lips pucker and press gently against his head. I let him rest on my mouth, peppering the tip with slow, pouty kisses, sucking him gently, gradually between my lips. My tongue glides along the length of his cock as I work him down my throat until I can take no more. He arches his back and moves his hand to the back of my head, holding me in place.

My hips shift forward, pussy throbbing as my breathing pauses, his cock deep in my throat. I start to move my hand between my thighs but look up at him pleadingly before continuing. He nods down at me and I quickly cup my mound over my jeans, my fingertips probing between my lips through the coarse cloth.

His grip on my hair loosens and I slide him out of my mouth enough to catch my breath. My clit catches between my finger and the seam of my jeans, and a spasm of pleasure rolls through me. My eyes flutter closed and I moan, taking his cock inside me again, beginning to work him rhythmically with my mouth.

There's the sound of furniture stirring across the floor behind me. Out of the corner of my eye, I see that Hal has repositioned a love seat to face us and is seated, absentmindedly fondling his cock through his pants. Like some sort of perverse Pavlovian response, watching Hal incites me to tease James more. I alternate between sucking him deep and hard at a slow, steady pace and then switching over to swirling my tongue around his head and down his shaft.

James is leaning against the counter using both hands now, rocking slightly from my ministrations. I wrap one hand around the base of his penis, guiding him between my lips, while my other hand is planted firmly over my cunt, working against the fabric to build my orgasm.

My body is thrumming with excitement, beyond sensitive to every shift of my tank top against my nipples, every muscle tensing in my thighs, every indication of my climax approaching.

I lose myself in the sensations, eyes closed and moaning around his cock in my mouth, ready to shudder with orgasmic relief. Without warning, he reaches down and grips my hair sharply. I look up in surprise, cock still between my lips, my orgasm suspended on the edge.

"Not yet."

Somehow, his refusal almost sends me past the point of no return but I restrain myself, hand on my pussy slowing to a crawl as I draw out my pleasure. I continue thrusting him into my mouth, more greedily now as I ride the edge of my orgasm.

I hear moans and whimpers that take me a minute to recognize as my own.

After a few minutes of blissful torment, Hal pipes up. "Let her finish. She can do this all day."

Grateful, I glance over at him. His hard cock is firmly in hand, though he's barely stroking himself, just focusing on watching us instead. My eyes shift up to James's, pleading wordlessly as the tip of my tongue darts along the junction of his head and shaft.

He grunts his approval down at me and I take him inside me to the hilt as my fingers reach a blazing pace on my clit and finally, finally, my orgasm tumbles through me. Screaming wordlessly, filled completely, I come, gasping for air between moans. He holds my head in place as the pleasure spreads through my cunt and only lets go when I'm suddenly, inexplicably, having difficulty supporting my trembling body.

His cock slides out of my mouth as he reaches down and gathers me up in his arms. The burst of pleasure is subsiding, and he kisses me gently until it ebbs completely. I'm amazed at how hard I've come, and we've only just begun. That realization and, less subtly, his hand groping at my ass, bring me back into the moment with a renewed throb of lust in my center.

Smiling, I break away from the kiss and stand up on tiptoes slightly to pause near his ear. "Thank you, James. May I have another?" I whisper before nibbling at his neck. He clutches my ass firmly, cupping my cheeks and crushing me into his body. His cock twitches against my mound, my jeans already soaked through along the seam. He reaches between us to confirm this with a satisfied smirk. His fingers stroke me from ass to clit, slowly and methodically. I squirm but he holds me still, his lips teasing mine.

He steps back to undo my pants, crouching as he slides them and my panties down. Even the rustle of fabric over my clit makes me shiver, though not as much as his breath against my shaved pussy does. He pauses, looking me over and bracing my ass with his hands, before lowering his lips to my cunt. A single kiss makes me sigh before he slides his tongue between my lips to the entrance of my pussy and laps upward.

The sensations almost overwhelm me, my body reacting strongly to his touch. I arc my hips forward, giving him easier access, and he repeats the motion with his tongue, slow and deliberate.

My hands run over his scalp, nails trailing and clutching at him with each stroke. I'm too wound up; my legs are unstable, even with him supporting my ass. He picks up on my uncertainty when his next stroke actually causes my knees to buckle momentarily.

He looks up at me, grinning, before standing back up and motioning for me to step out of the pants still encircling my ankles. He joins me in shedding that layer of clothing and when we're finished, he reaches behind me, grips my ass and thighs and lifts me in the air. My legs wrap around him without hesitation, and I can feel the length of his cock pressing against my pussy and ass.

"Fuck," I mutter out loud without intending to. Feeling him so close, so hard, is torment all over again.

"Yeah?" he responds, still grinning. He digs his fingers into my ass and starts sliding my wet pussy back and forth over his cock, but not putting it inside yet.

"God-fucking-damn." The list goes on as I verbalize my frustrations. He cuts me off with a kiss and swings us around, taking a few steps before lowering me to the ground. As he lowers me, his cock glides between my lips, over my clit, until it is pressed against my mound again.

I'm about to continue my verbal abuse when he spins me

around and bends me over on the back of a conveniently placed, comfortably padded chair in front of me. Hal is seated on the love seat directly across from us, still stroking himself lazily, though a bit more firmly now. His eyes are watching me intensely.

James's hands slide up my back, underneath my tank top, before moving back down to my ass, smoothing over each globe and then spreading my cheeks. I grip the chair, watching Hal's cock slide between his fingers.

Releasing my ass, James moves his hands down over my thighs, all the way to my calves and ankles, kneeling in the process. He shifts my legs apart even more, so I'm fully spread before him. Gripping my ass again, my cheeks spread, he starts licking trails along my thigh to my glistening lips. I lean down more and he buries his face in my pussy.

His tongue starts at my clit, teasing the pert button, and then drags through the path between my lips, sliding inside me for a second. He repeats this, occasionally slicking his tongue around my asshole, making me squirm and back toward him.

My eyes remain trained on Hal the entire time, watching him stroke himself with more intensity as my own orgasm builds. Seeing his pleasure growing as I moan under James's touch makes my pulse and cunt throb in unison.

I feel James pull away from me briefly and almost turn to see what has happened when he slips a finger inside me smoothly. I moan, eyes fluttering closed of their own accord, and then moan again more loudly as he adds another finger on his next stroke. He presses against my G-spot briefly, then adds yet another finger, my pussy accommodating it gladly. He thrusts inside me, increasing his pace slowly.

My muscles tense and contract around his fingers as he brings me to a shuddering orgasm. As I come, cunt gushing, I open my eyes and see Hal stroking himself furiously, watching me scream only a few feet away from him. My legs give out beneath me, and I grasp at the chair even though I'm safely supported by it.

I'm still riding out the end of my orgasm when James's fingers slide out of me and his mouth returns to my clit. He laps at me expertly, deliberately and hungrily. After the attention on my G-spot, my clit is charged with sensation and a finger thrust sneakily into my ass sets me off again.

I scream his name, Hal's, and those of every deity I can think of as my body bucks in pleasure. He keeps the pace up as long as my pussy can take it, my orgasm lasting for what feels like hours and very well may be by the look on Hal's face when I open my eyes again. He's stopped stroking himself and is instead just circling his finger over the head of his penis.

James has stilled behind me, and their sudden quiet snaps me out of my postorgasm glow.

"Fuck her," Hal states plainly, eyes locked on mine. Not a question, a demand.

I grip the chair, shaking with anticipation from his statement. I hear James shift behind me and then one hand is on my hip, the other pushing my back down lower onto the chair so my ass is high in the air.

The head of his cock brushes my clit lightly before he arcs his pelvis and thrusts inside me in one stroke. I moan as his girth fills me and my pussy twitches around him. I keep my eyes on Hal, who is stroking himself again, sitting on the edge of the love seat now.

James thrusts into me, slowly, teasingly, tapping against my G-spot, pulling out, then barely sliding back inside for a few strokes before filling me again. My hips rock to the rhythm he's setting, arching back toward him in an effort to drive him inside me farther.

A sharp slap on my ass is James's response to my attempts. Not exactly a deterrent, to be perfectly honest, but I take the hint and try to stay still. It's becoming increasingly difficult, as my body is already building toward an orgasm, which my moans make very obvious.

Hal shakes his head.

"Harder," he instructs James, watching my reaction.

James slams inside me, making me cry out. He pauses between strokes but increases the amount of force with each one. I fight my orgasm, trying to ignore the pressure mounting at my core; ignore the way Hal is stroking himself, matching James's thrusts; ignore the wetness dripping down my thighs.

"Faster." My eyes close as his tempo speeds up and I bite my lip, willing myself to control my reactions. My head drops as his thrusts move me over the chair, barely supporting myself anymore, simply being fucked, hard and fast.

James grunts behind me and reaches forward to grab my hair, wrenching me up to face Hal again, arching my body so it's impossible not to feel every deep stroke against my G-spot.

I can't hold it any longer. Hal knows it. He has a half smile on his face as I come against his wishes. My pussy squeezes James's cock inside me, my screams drowning out everything else around me. He lets go of my hair as my body bucks wildly. The orgasm rips through me and then fades to a pleasant plateau of more to come, but the thrusts don't slow down or let up as I anticipated. By the way James is gripping my hips, the cadence of his grunts, I realize he's not just following orders.

He's fucking me hard and fast because that's exactly what he wants to do.

I raise my head, still recovering but feeling a surge rising in me again already. Whether that's a good thing is unclear though, based on the expression on Hal's face.

I think I'm about to be taught a lesson on the importance of following orders.

Hal leans back onto the love seat, legs askew, cock erect in one hand and the other raising to beckon me over.

Propping myself up as best I can under the pounding I'm still taking, I look over my shoulder at James. He's completely engrossed in what he's doing, which, as that's me, makes me hate to interrupt him. He notices the shift in my pose and looks down at me, then over at Hal before realizing what he's requesting.

Attempting to appear nonchalant, with only a hint of sadness in his expression, he runs his hands over my back to my ass before stepping away. My pussy is drenched, and he runs his penis over my ass as he leans over to help me stand up again.

Gaining my footing, I give his cock a quick squeeze before walking over to Hal.

I'm standing right in front of him and he points brusquely at my tank top, motioning for me to take it off. I do so, tossing it over my shoulder in James's direction.

"Hey!" he mutters, but trails off.

Hal beckons again, and I move in closer, one knee on the sofa as I lean in for a kiss. He doesn't move, doesn't even really look at me and I second-guess his intentions a moment too late. His hand reaches up and snatches me by the neck, guiding me directly in front of his gaze.

"I thought I said no."

I don't move. I don't blink. I don't do anything obvious that could aggravate this any more. I do, however, feel my pussy tense in anticipation.

He knows me too well. My innocent act doesn't fool him, and he smirks at my attempt. His fingers tighten until I whimper.

"I'm sorry," I squeak out. He pushes me back until I'm standing again before letting go.

"No, you're not. But you will be."

He grabs me by the arm and spins me around to face away from him. James is watching us, transfixed, cock twitching as he waits to see what's next.

"You're going to sit down, I'm going to fuck your ass and if you come, so help me..." Hal trails off. I nod, looking over my shoulder as I straddle him, positioning myself carefully. He's still fully dressed other than his penis peeking through his opened pants. I start to lower down and he grips my ass, guiding me across him, my juices soaking his cock. I shudder as he brushes my clit, then yelp as he slides swiftly down to prod my asshole.

He slips his head inside my ass and I bite my lip, closing my eyes and forcing my muscles to relax but somehow not relax enough for me to come in the process. He works inside me slowly as my asshole resists him, tight and unrelenting. Finally, he fills me and I breathe deeply, accommodating his thickness.

Despite the fact that I'm not supposed to come, out of habit my hand drops to my clit to tease myself until my ass relaxes around his cock. He slides in and out slowly, my muscles fluttering around him with each thrust and each stroke of my fingertip.

Hal's arm snakes around me and pulls me close against his chest, the buttons of his shirt scratching at my back pleasingly. My head rests against his shoulder and he grips both of my arms, holding me in place and preventing me from putting any attention on my clit as he speeds up the tempo.

I consider protesting and my eyes open to reveal that James is standing in front of us, cock in hand and a smile on his face.

"I think she deserves it," Hal grunts between thrusts.

I realize what they've decided I deserve, and a shiver runs through me. Hal slows his thrusting as James leans down and lifts my legs up, spreading me and giving himself easier access to my pussy. His cock nudges my clit and I buck without meaning to. I don't go very far with Hal still bracing my arms, but I'm having trouble controlling my reactions now, too excited to finally have them both filling me up.

James braces himself, using the back of the love seat as leverage, and slides inside my pussy. I moan and he grunts as my cunt constricts around him. I'm already so full, but my muscles relax enough for them to begin alternately thrusting inside me.

Hal slides out of my ass as James fills my pussy. I'm mindless from the sensations and they pump inside me relentlessly, their cocks drifting over each other inside me. They're grunting in time to their thrusts and James leans forward to kiss me, cupping the back of my head to bring me toward him. He bites and sucks on my lower lip, fucking me harder as our kiss intensifies. Hal's lips and tongue move along my neck, causing shivers on top of everything else.

My body feels like it's about to burst at the seams from their exertions and I'm moaning nonstop now, trying to somehow control the surging orgasm threatening to breach at any moment. I grip on to Hal's thigh, my nails digging into his flesh, and he gets the hint. His mouth moves up to beside my ear.

"Come."

They both fill me on the next stroke and I come, clamping down on their cocks, pussy and ass shuddering in relief. James's kiss drowns out my screams and I grip on to both of them as my body bucks in pleasure. Heat radiates from my cunt, spreading throughout my body, and my orgasm hits a plateau as they continue thrusting, before spiraling up to an even more intense explosion of pleasure.

My head falls back and Hal reaches up with one hand to cup my mouth as I scream in ecstasy. My vision blurs and I almost black out, but the constant drilling keeps me alert, if lost in sensation.

They're both grunting louder now, too, as my spasms work their cocks against each other, tighter with each stroke. James pulls out suddenly, spilling himself over my breasts, shooting streams of semen onto my body. Hal joins him moments later, coming inside my ass, his cock twitching as he spurts and his grip on me relaxing.

I'm too exhausted to do anything more than lie there, and apparently that goes for the boys as well. James collapses onto the nearby chair with a satisfied smile, and Hal wraps an arm around my waist.

After a few minutes of silence punctuated by heavy breathing, Hal reaches up and tweaks my nipple.

"Hey!" I exclaim, brushing his hand off. He slaps my thigh in response.

"Well, I was going to suggest a drink, but if you two are good to go again..." James trails off, and I can feel Hal's cock twitch inside me.

He's joking, right? I think to myself.

Looks like I'm wrong again.

BREATH

Mollena Williams

The man I serve is not the Prince Charming of my childhood fantasies. Neither is he the dominant I conjured up from my fevered imaginings once I uncovered the buried bunker that was my submissive self. He is, in fact, very fucking far away from those imaginary beings. What I sought was someone near me, someone single, also monogamous, available to be a part of every facet of my life. Instead I landed feet first and stunned out of my right mind by a man who was quite polyamorous, already happily married and most of the continent away from where I lived. My brain and my powers of rational reasoning were sure that this was a situation that would never, ever take root. That it was impossible, outside of my desires, a terrible compromise. His smile, his confidence and the way he silenced the chorus of naysayers in my head within moments of pushing me into a corner and whispering into my ear turned the tide. His voice—cinnamon molasses, burnt honey and twilight—calmed me into relaxing my guard a bit. Just a bit, but that was all he needed. I found myself a shaking, loose-limbed rag doll, gazing unblinking into the depths of his eyes, green and sparkling and dangerous and delicious, and I knew that saying no to him was simply not an option...and never would be.

In our play, he was always very personal. Though skilled with the whip and cane, and handy with rope and restraints and all manner of sharp, shiny danger, he preferred to use his hands. "I like to know it is me hurting you"—his voice slipped into my head and elicited my own slow smile—"because I enjoy that direct control far, far more than having an implement between us."

Agreed. His hands are, after all, so expressive. So descriptive.

The first time I found his hands around my throat, I had a combined sensation of arousal and panic. I have a rather negative reaction to my breathing being cut off that way: it causes immediate headache and blinding pain. The first time this happened, he immediately went into triage mode to ensure I was okay. Submitting to an ER nurse has its upside. Deciding that the risk wasn't worth it, he moved on to other excruciating torments. And let me tell you, nurses can be some sadistic motherfuckers—also an upside, as far as I am concerned.

Since our relationship is long distance, the times when we do see each other feel heightened. There is so much to balance; his wife, other partners and the brevity of our time together serve to add weight and urgency to every encounter. So when I was able to see him again, after some absence, and look forward to playing with him, every aspect of my emotional, physical and mental selves was poised and sharpened.

This particular event was held, as so many kink events are, in a hotel. I found myself on the floor in a playspace that had been assembled thanks to the labor and intentions of a close-knit group of people who run the event. My dominant is one of them, and so taking time off from the work of running an event to stop and play is a precious connection indeed.

There isn't anything particularly special about a hotel ballroom. And there sure as hell wasn't anything special about the hideous carpeting in said ballroom.

But there is magic when you realize that you are being pushed into the aforementioned hideous carpet and you feel every inch of skin being abraded against it as you writhe on the floor, trying to breathe.

I was past coherency. I didn't think about anything clearly except how it was becoming more and more difficult to inhale. I was surprised to learn that my previous issues with breath-play had been neatly circumvented. I was aroused to see him smiling at me, calmly, as I struggled for breath.

How did I wind up in a breath-play scene? Why can't I breathe? He isn't choking me... What is happening? Oh, god.

This did not start out as a breath-play scene at all. It started out with one of my favorite toys, a flexible-handled cat-o'-nine-tails. A thuddy whip will get my attention every time. We'd started out with a silly opening to our scene, a playful teasing series of orders to strip, which I obeyed with a faux reluctance, a wink and a smile. The long crimson and saffron scarf that floated about my shoulders wound around my throat as I found the other end of it wound around his hand, but of course he wouldn't strangle me with it...that was off the table.

Warm-up consisted of the whip finding its flicker-tongued way across the back of my thighs, eliciting sighs and squeals alike from me. But there was an odd impermanence to the rhythm and before long he had put down the whip in favor of availing himself of my pain with his hands.

Fair enough, I thought, since his hands are fairly fucking formidable. This thought was followed by my wailing scream as he dug his fingers deep into the big muscles of my thighs, fingers pushing with insane force into the crease where my hip socket hid within muscle and tendons, pushing me to the place where speech becomes an eel in my mouth and I can't quite manage words, stuttering and spitting syllables to beg for... what? Mercy? That is a fucking laugh because when I start to feel that real pain; when I can see him observing the edges of my composure fraying: it is just getting good, and mercy simply isn't in the cards.

I was hiccupping and writhing away from him, trying to escape the thrumming pain in my muscles as he squeezed, compressed and pulled them to places where my wordless verbalizing became a stream of shouts and moans, and I think if you'd been there and closed your eyes you might have thought you were front row in the amen corner of your friendly neighborhood Pentecostal church. Except I wasn't even trying to pretend the ecstasy and the surreal glossolalia were due to anything but unrelenting pain and protracted torment at the hands of someone I trusted completely. And as the pain became more intense, my body's energy and charge around pain focused it to a shaking climax that wracked me, again and again, as I felt myself break apart and resolve into a heaving panting orgasmic response.

And then my hiccupping breath escaped me.

And failed to return.

I tried again to inhale and found myself strangely desperate for breath. Not in a wheezy asthmatic way. Not in that stabbing-pressure-to-my-head, strangulation way. I just...couldn't inhale. And I couldn't figure out why. I blinked and connected solidly with him as he observed my face, looking into my eyes and no doubt seeing my confusion. He leaned in closer to me and I realized then I couldn't breathe properly because his arm was between us, aligned underneath my breasts, compressing my rib cage evenly. No pain, no muss, no fuss—but I couldn't. Fucking. Breathe.

I put my hand against his chest, at first with a sort of pleading flutter rather than roughly pushing him away. And he backed off.

For a moment.

I caught my breath and took in as much air as I could, only to feel him leaning in again, face inches away from mine, and I could feel my heart squirming in my chest, lungs shuddering, diaphragm confounded in its standard action. My body had been doing this job for just over forty-two years and hadn't previously encountered an external force that bothered to interfere with it in this way. But here it was, and there he went, pressing again with a force that was almost gentle and didn't hurt, not really, but terrified me all the more because I felt my vision narrowing and a small white-hot panic blossom behind my eyes. I'd only felt this type of diminishing of my faculties once before, and that was a very bad moment. I had feared then that I might be dying and now that same genie erupted from the bottle and the thought occurred to my confused mind that the logical result of him continuing on the path we were currently exploring was my suffocation.

I shoved him as hard as I could, gaining another lungful of air and another opportunity to vent my slipstream of confusion as I watched him watching me and he permitted me this struggle, as I twisted away and dragged myself a few feet before he brought me back and pulled me over and under him and pushed down on me again and I sobbed. Shaking, I felt my chest relax, strangely, as he leaned in again and pushed.

And again.

And again.

The cycle of resistance was winding down. I was drained—drained, and impossibly aroused. Even as I whined and suffocated, my cunt was wet. With a shift in his leg, he pressed himself more closely to me. I could feel his cock and knew my suffering was feeding him, too.

Even as I was dimming, he was feeding, and I luxuriated in being drained—drained and trapped in his eyes as I watched him watch me fading, saw his eyes dilate even as my eyes drifted shut and I moaned, my hand no longer pushing him away, but instead resting on his arm. I let go. I did not hurt and my panic had died into a sweet terror...not of him, though.

I wondered what it might be like to have the last thing I saw be his eyes on mine, that barely visible smile, lips parted to inhale the last wisps of breath that escaped mine. I lost my desire to fight. In that moment I remember one thought, swimming upward from the murky depths of my consciousness...the thought that I did not need to fight him. Fighting him was not what I wanted, never what I wanted. What I wanted was to graciously, gratefully endure whatever he gave me. And as I gave him that, my wordless pleas again becoming manifestations of the slippery, beautiful terror, I was so totally his that I let go of myself and gave myself to him. And there was nothing, nothing at all in those moments that would have driven me to assert my will against his.

Not even the will to breathe.

The heat of his gaze as he took in my acquiescence, my submission to this torment, suffused me, his energy surging even as mine ebbed and oh, such sweetness...

Then I *was* breathing again. Then I was in his arms, safe from him. Safe with him. Then there were tears, and then there was more. Then I lacked words and took his hand in my hands and pressed his hand to my lips, over and over again.

I crawled up and knelt at his feet, sobbing and wet and shaken and his.

Everything I could say about those moments, that conversation we had without words, all of it sounds like hyperbolic histrionics. There are ways and there are ways that power exchange manifests. Manifesting power to give control of my autonomous functions to another human being...and to do so voluntarily, to look into the eyes of another person and give him everything is a sweet emotional narcotic.

And I am fully addicted.

SILVER FISH IN THE CRYSTAL POOL

Gina Marie

Later, he will tell me that he thought about that scene, planned it, choreographed it to the smallest detail. He knew when I would whimper, when I would beg, when I would twist against the bark and spread my quivering legs. Later, he will grin and lick his lips and tell me how beautiful I looked in the sunshine, how when I collapsed backward against the ropes, then forward into his arms, I made an ethereal, animalistic sound, like an angel being fucked by the devil.

But right now it's happening, and so intense, so immediate, so raw that I can barely express what it feels like. We're out in the weeds and the trees on the dry side of the mountain. Ponderosa country. The air is hot and dry and smells of branches and dust, the vanilla of ponderosa sap, the bitter salt of sweat, come, pheromones and thick, sweet musk rising.

"The tree has my name on it," Alec says, grinning like a boy and looking it up and down, giving it a loving pat on the belly, tapping me gently on the ass.

"This is a perfect tree for the tree whore."

My tree is sturdy and rough. The bark is warm against my skin. I can smell the pine oil in my tree's exhalations. My tree. My lover. My ropes and buckles and straps.

My lover knows what I want and why I want it. He knows that the sun on my flesh is like food, that his lips against my blinded face and muted mouth are like fire that stokes my soul into believing that all things are possible. He knows that pain is pleasure and that my need to walk on the steep edge of it is marrow deep. Alec strips me naked in the sunshine and begins teasing my flesh. Our skin begins to melt in the heat, and our bodies become indistinguishable from each other.

Before Alec wraps the scarf around my eyes, he buckles the thick vinyl cuffs around my wrists. The sound of metal and vinyl, the smell of it heating up in the sun and against my damp skin makes me weak. I can feel my clit pulsing in the warm breeze. I can smell the molten core of my earth, bark and moss and spore, as it is lifted gently by the wind in the trees.

A creek gurgles in the distance, "Let go, let go, let go, let go."

Next, my lover binds my torso and legs, the bark hot and harsh against my naked ass and back. He can't stop grinning. He knows. He knows I have lived every day of my life for these few moments.

The blindfold is next. Suddenly, summertime is gone and I am left to dangle there in the wind and birdsong and creek babble, a feeling like floating and being tied to the tracks all at once. I hear a gentle rattle and feel a sharp pain on my nipples as soft fingers clamp them between a heavy metal chain. Then follows a sharp pain between my legs as he places rubber-tipped clamps on my swollen labia. My head swings sideways, hair clinging to the bark. The disembodied "he" is ready with a strip of tape that he presses firmly across my mouth with his large hands, then he tugs on the chain as he moves the whip handle between my legs.

The whip doesn't strike, it strokes. At first. The soft-as-silk elk-hide fringes feather across my skin like a thousand butterfly kisses. The darkened sky is comforting as he brushes my ears and neck with his lips and whispers dirty, dirty words that make my nipples burn.

The next puff of wind catches a drop of wetness winding down my thigh. The sensation of it traveling across my skin—this tiny but significant offering to the sex gods—makes my legs begin to shake.

The whip comes down hard on my belly, my breasts, my thighs, my pussy. The sting and scent of leather, skin and my own excitement cause a chemical reaction and my blood is replaced with surging electrical currents.

I jolt against the ropes. I am moaning into the tape. And then everything stops. Silence, except for the sound of air rushing in and out of my nose, the wind in the branches, a twig underfoot. Minutes go by and nothing happens. I am dripping into the pine duff, every sense on alert for the next electric zap, whip strike, kiss. The next sensation is the whip handle sliding between my legs. Suddenly, swiftly, the tape is off my mouth and the taste of me is on my tongue, the leather handle wet with my juice and pressed against my lips, hard and wet. Very wet. He pulls it back and forth across my mouth. The drop of wetness on my thigh is now a rivulet, a cool little river of come leading from the mountains to the ocean.

And then the world stands still with this one whispered sentence, the sentence that flays me more harshly than any whip or clamp or hand. His fingers flutter against me when he says it, reaching deep inside. "You're not wet, lover. Why aren't you wet?" The breeze catches the river of juice streaming down my thighs and my mind is tumbling.

"I am so wet," I stutter, my lips now unbound but clumsy. "I am so wet."

"No, no you're not, baby. Don't you like this? Doesn't this feel good?"

"Oh, it feels so good, so good."

"I don't believe you. You're not wet. Do you want to come, baby? Do you? Well, you can't come until you're wet. Don't I make you wet?"

My heart is racing as Alec flogs my thighs, pulls my head sideways by my ponytail and inflicts small, sharp bites on my neck and breasts. A woodpecker knocks wood in a nearby tree. Something, probably a pinecone, falls and bounces in a stinging glance off my bare shoulder. He tugs at the labia clamps and pushes me to my knees, shoving his cock deep into my throat. "Maybe this is what you need," he growls, his voice the red-hot interior of a rumbling volcano.

My brain, a lightning storm of desire, is consumed by the length of him, smooth and warm, stretching my lips. My knees are grinding in the pine needle duff as he pushes himself deeper and deeper, pulling out just long enough to allow me a drooling, gasping breath. I strain at the cuffs, wanting to wrap my arms around his muscular ass, feel the heat rippling across his skin.

He shoves his cock in deep and holds it there against the song of my throat for an eternity. Juice is streaming down my legs. Wet, so fucking wet.

He is tugging on the nipple clamps. I am straining into the cuffs. My desire is as big as the sky. I am upside down. Not wet? Not wet? Lips on my neck. Hands between my legs. Nipples taut and burning. Not wet?

Alec fingers my clit again, pulls on the labia chain, bites at my nipples. I fall forward against his chest and scream against the ropes. Pain and pleasure flash in the sweat-soaked wilderness of my mind.

"Mmmm," he says, slapping my ass and smacking his lips, shoving his pussy-soaked hand into my mouth. "That's more like it. About time you got excited. About time you got wet. About time you got ready for me."

Orgasm hardly matters anymore as shadow figures, voices, chants, growls, whispers, chains, slaps, leather sting and the thrust of silicone cock and vibration of thick, smooth plastic take over my body. But I come, oh I do. I come and come and come again, in my mind, in my mouth, my clit, my cunt, my heart, my head. He is in me now, sending me spinning from the inside out, master and mind, body and brain. I am spinning through space, the owl at dusk, the deer bounding in and out of dawn, the silver fish spinning in the crystal pool.

At last, I collapse against the ropes and scream so loud I don't recognize the sound of my own ecstasy.

As soon as Alex releases me from my binds, I reach between my legs to feel it for myself, the quenched thirst of a thousand sunflowers blooming in the desert. My fingers emerge, glistening, from my own pussy. I wipe myself across his temple and swat at his ass. "You!" I exclaim. "You are *so* bad...not wet."

Later he will chuckle and nibble at my ear. "Sure had you going."

"You sure did," I will reply, a dark, damp spot spreading into my jeans at the steakhouse after work. "You sure did."

THE SECRET OF TIME TRAVEL

Jacqueline Applebee

I am black. My lover is white. I call him Sir, partly out of respect, but mostly because it makes him smile. We are each other's opposite in many ways. I have short hair that curls tight against my head. Sir's hair is long and fair; it swishes down his back when he bends to kiss me. His every thought can be seen in his bright blue eyes. No one knows what I am thinking when they look into my brown ones. I am an unlikely incident. I am smaller than I seem. Sir is huge when he stands over me. There is no question that I love him.

I've been working as a community debt adviser for over five years now. We get the ones who nobody else will touch, the shopkeepers who lost it all in the riots last summer, the alcoholics who couldn't hold it together. We deal with all the shit that blows through the door.

Mister Munroe had twenty-seven credit cards. He used to run a chain of takeaways on the south coast. Ever eat a chicken kebab in Bournemouth? That would probably be one of his. But then Mister Munroe's wife left him. He started letting things slip. Debt collectors surrounded him like the vultures they are. They picked him clean, leaving nothing behind but worthless plastic. Mister Munroe's health went the same way as his kebab shops. He was in my office this morning shaking with tears. I only managed to get three debt collecting agencies off his back, but it gave us the time we needed. Time is something I'm interested in; time travel in particular is a hobby of mine. My antique silver pocket watch is a constant reminder that time is precious, but I have undeniable proof that time can be twisted, bent and forced back in on itself. I know the secret, you see.

Sir has wide flat hands. His veins are blue beneath his skin. He takes off his belt, looping it over his knuckles. I feel myself getting wet; everything starts to tingle. My knickers are white with little hearts dotted all over. They are soaked by the time my lover taps his belt impatiently against his thigh. He watches me as I push my knickers down. My brown skin is moisturized with smoky shea butter. I wonder if it is that or my arousal he can smell when I see him sniff the air.

Sir often wears aftershave with notes of cinnamon, cloves and other spices I cannot name. I always think of Christmas when he is near. I reach up on tiptoes, kiss him on the cheek. He smiles, and then he presses me back against the nearest wall. "You cannot get round me that way," he says. "Little girls need a firm hand."

"But I've been good," I complain, my voice a whisper.

My lover's hand whips out to hold me roughly by the chin. I feel my eyes prickle with sensation. There is a potential for tears of pain or joy. It's all down to Sir. He leans closer, his voice a hiss. "Do not lie to me."

* * *

I hate chopping onions. I'm a lover of gadgets but there aren't any that actually work at Lola's place. Lola has been my friend since we were both kids; as the only black children in our school, we were both exotic novelties. We were naturally drawn together. Our friendship has lasted throughout the years.

Lola collects men like trading cards; she's got a guaranteed shag waiting for her in every London borough except Tower Hamlets. The rest of her life is chaotic. I try to ignore the brown envelopes stacked on a shelf by the sink, but I already know what's inside every one of them.

Lola pounds a ball of dough. Her arms are strong and smooth. We're having poppy seed bread with our dinner. Quite surprisingly, a naked man walks in, raises his hand in greeting and then fills the kettle with water. I don't know where to look. I wipe my eyes, try not to slice my face with the knife.

Lola calls out over her shoulder, "Tommy, this is Jennifer."

Tommy holds out his hand, shakes mine with enthusiasm. "Oh, the money girl." He tilts his head. "That's awesome. Smart is so sexy, you know?" I feel Tommy's eyes rake over me. Even though he's the one with no clothes on, I suddenly feel extremely vulnerable. I try not to look down, but my gaze is drawn to his cock. He's getting hard. I turn away, attack the pile of potatoes with a shaking hand. "See you later maybe?" Tommy asks. I say nothing, hold myself still.

I try to distract myself with the food smells that waft about my head. It must have worked, as I jump when Lola comes up behind me. "Tommy's got a friend who's just flown over from the States. We could all go out together."

"I don't think so," I mutter.

Lola sighs dramatically. "I forgot you're only interested in kinky old blokes."

Lola never used to be this way. I don't know when she became so judgmental.

Sir beats me with fast light swats. His belt makes a whooshing noise as he moves. I giggle; I can't help myself. This is how I always respond at first.

"What are you laughing at, girl?" He tickles my side. "What's so funny?"

I squirm, wriggle with delight. I feel like a happy little soul. My lover's fingers are like fireworks. I crackle and sparkle when he touches me. The room glows bright with color.

"Silly little thing." He suddenly throws down his belt. He uses his hand instead. Sir's blows are hard and solid on my bottom. My breathing slows as I suck in big gulps of air. This is the second stage of my arousal. All the noise in my throat stops as I absorb the feel of his hand.

"You still with me?" he asks, bending his head to look at me. I nod, unable to speak. My voice escaped me a little while ago. My mind moves back in time to a place where everything was warm and snug; sensation was all I knew. My body follows with every breath I take. The secret of time travel is simply my lover's hand on my skin. Each impact of flesh against flesh pulls me into a sparkling vortex. Adventure lies beyond a curtain of pain.

I finish chopping vegetables for the stew. Lola covers the speckled bread dough, puts it in a warm place to rise. She pulls me up to her bedroom. "Come help me pick out a dress for tonight."

Lola's wardrobe is like an archive. She never throws anything away. Fashion has a habit of repeating itself every so often, so she always manages to look good. My friend strips down to her bra and knickers. We pick four possible dresses out of a bulging closet.

"Say you'll come with me tonight, Jennifer."

"I'm busy." I hold up a purple lace dress.

Lola scowls. "It's not healthy, honey. You're a grown woman, and you spend all your time subjugating yourself to this man. It's as if feminism never happened for you."

"Don't start on me."

"I mean how ancient is that guy you're seeing?"

"I'm actually a few years older than he is." Sir may be young in years, but he is very mature. It's not an act when we are together. Time travel goes in two directions for us. Where I regress, become little and sweet, my lover grows stern and domineering like nobody's business.

Lola pulls on the lace dress. "This might do. I've got a hat that will be killer with this." She turns this way and that, admiring herself in the long mirror fixed to the wardrobe door. But then I see something else reflected. Tommy creeps into the room. He is still stark naked. He pounces on Lola. They both topple to the bed. Lola laughs at the top of her lungs as he holds her down. I am trapped, unable to make a getaway. I don't want to see this. I squeeze my eyes shut, cover my ears. Behind the red-black of my eyelids I see myself as a child, cowering, trying to hide as my babysitter forced me to watch a porn film. I could not escape. I could not look away. This is an occasion when time travel is unexpected, totally undesired. I don't always want to journey to the past. It isn't all sunshine and roses back there.

Sir directs me to kneel. I feel positively tiny as he sits on a chair. His fingers go to his fly. I listen to the metallic rasp as the zipper slides down. I feel heavy. I feel solid and real. Sir's cock is pinker than the rest of him. It is smooth and hard as he rubs it against my face. My lips stretch around the salt-sticky tip. Everything goes out of focus as I move my mouth down, down, as far as I can go. I feel the murmur Sir makes as he relaxes inside me. I raise my head a little and watch, entranced, as my saliva shimmers in the light. Sir holds my head, pushes me back down very gently. I go the rest of the way on my own. My hand strokes over his thighs. I feel the texture of his fine linen trousers. This is the third way I respond. Words don't exist, vision is meaningless. All that is left is taste and touch and sound. It's as far back as I can go before I disappear into nothingness. My lover's cock bumps against the back of my throat. His curly pubic hair brushes against my nose. It is the only part of him that is even remotely soft. It feels good that I am able to feel it. I want to swallow him whole. I want to keep him inside me, deep down where he can never leave. My nipples hurt with a good hurt. One of my hands leaves his thighs so I can pinch and play with myself. Sir makes a sighing noise. His cock gets even harder against my tongue.

"Good girl," he says. "You're my good girl."

I feel his words instead of hearing them. It is everything I need. The resonance of his voice circles my labia. My clitoris pulses hard. It is enough to make me come. Sir grips my head with his wide, gentle hands. He jerks against me, spurting inside my mouth. Everything bitter tastes wonderful to me. I drink him down, keep him inside me for as long as I can. I rest my head against his knee. There is no question that I love him.

Tommy pulls the dress right off Lola's back, ripping the fabric as he moves. I'm frozen in place as he straddles her. My feet refuse to move. I can hardly breathe. Tommy holds his cock, looks over at me with a smirk, and then he shoves inside her. I feel sick. I want to run, but the door seems miles away. Finally my feet move, one slow footstep after the other. Soon I am through the open door. I race to the bathroom, clutching my pocket watch to my chest, but it clatters to the floor. I tumble inside the cold room, gasping. I go to shut the door but a hand stops me.

Tommy calls out. "Are you okay, Jennifer?"

My hand falters on the doorknob. Part of me wants to slam the door shut on his fingers, but I can't do it. The moment's hesitation is all it takes for the naked man to widen the gap and squeeze inside the bathroom with me.

"Please put some clothes on." I turn to face the windows.

I feel a wave of heat as Tommy moves closer. I can smell my friend's scent on his skin. He was inside her not two minutes ago.

"Being naked shouldn't scare you," Tommy says as if he's speaking to a simpleton. "And when you've got what I've got, why should I keep it to myself?"

I turn to face him, incredulous. "Get out."

Tommy tilts his head. "You're not shy, are you?" He gestures over his shoulder. "Lola's not. In fact, she's quite adventurous. We both want you to come to bed."

My eyes dart to the door. "I don't believe you."

Tommy snorts. "Who do you think sent me to fetch you?" He moves even closer. "She set the whole thing up, cross my heart and hope to die." He grins at me, showing sharp teeth. "Stick a needle in my eye."

I back against the washbasin. My fingers touch the porcelain but then they curl around something cold, hard and pointed. A pair of scissors is in my grip before I know it. I hold it up, aware of how my hand shakes.

Tommy smirks at me. "You ain't got the nerve. Lola told me how you like to get off playing the innocent little girl." He leans forward. His breath touches me as a chill. I try not to shiver, but I'm frozen with fear. "You just want a real man to take control, don't you?"

I angle the scissors so it points directly at his cock. Tommy swallows, and then he backs out of the room without another word. After a few minutes I creep outside. I spot the glint of my pocket watch on the hallway floor. I almost cry with relief as I pick it up. I storm out of the house, slamming the door behind me. I'm an innocent little girl for Sir alone. Everyone else can fuck right off.

This is how it always ends. Sir wipes my face with a big white hanky. He pours me a glass of orange juice. Things come back into focus once the sugar hits my system. My lover holds me as I cry a little. I'm never sad at what we do; I'm crying because I can. I'm crying because it is safe to be small with him.

Time deposits me back to the present day. I am a weary, happy traveler. Sir digs out an ancient videotape of cartoons when I am able to sit up on my own. We sit cross-legged on the floor; share a bowl of popcorn, half sweet, half salty. We both laugh at the silly antics onscreen. I check my pocket watch after a while. I will the seconds to halt, but it doesn't work for me. I know it is time to leave.

"Next Saturday?" Sir asks as I pull on my coat.

"Sounds good."

My lover kisses me on the cheek. "Who's my sweetie?"

"I am," I say with a smile. "I love you."

I step into my heels, feeling a little strange at my sudden elevation. I walk outside and hail a cab. I journey home across London, checking my email on my futuristic phone. I eat dinner, and then do a little research for Mister Munroe's remaining debts. I am totally grown up and responsible. I am an adult. But for Sir, the hands of the clock go back at his command. I am forever his good little girl.

BARED

Gray Miller

It is dark. There is no subtle mood lighting, no moonlight, no sharp diagonal streetlight cast on the wall through a slitted shade. It is black in the bedroom, the bed and chair and dresser hidden. Even the usual contrast of their skin—her rich chocolate against his pale cream—remains unseen. Everything is by touch, by sound and by breath, catching, hissing, grunting as they move together.

Foreplay is not the stroking of gentle fingers along the back, or the kiss of soft lips against neck. Foreplay is the rough dishevelment of clothing almost ripped off, of teeth bared and muscles flexed in the violent pursuit of pleasure. Tonight is rope and sweat, strong hands pulling her body this way and that, twisting her arms behind and tightly strapping her forearms together. Her chest thrusts forward, naked tits swollen and heavy from his hard grasp, nipples taut with longing. He surrounds them with rope, over and under, fingers pinching as they pass over the points, her moans adding a soft melody to the rhythm of their bodies moving with and against each other. Other nights he suckles her breasts almost reverently. This night he feasts on them, drawing as much into his mouth as he can, then pulling back, thickening nipple captured between soft tongue and hard teeth. He bites hard, harder, more than most could take, but she is feral and a growl rises from deep in her throat. It escalates into a throaty cry as her head flies back, teeth flashing as she drinks in the dark joy of the pain made pleasure. This is love, yes, but this is not sweet. They are reaching for the animal, the deep, the primal, extracting the pleasure with violent struggle.

Strong fingers pull at her waistband, ripping the delicate lace from her hips. He slides them across the slick wetness of her hot and swollen cunt. Two fingers plunge deep with a come-hither motion again and again, causing her hips to buck with longing, sharp breath gasping out a low murmuring, "Yes..." He echoes the word back, intoxicated by the feeling of her strong body under his hands, his mouth. She pushes up, harder, until it seems it is his hand that is captured, enveloped over and over, by the driving urgency of her cunt. His cock presses against her leg as he fingers her, thumb pressing her mons as her hips piston up against the web of his hand. He begins slow circles around her clit, fingers pressing harder, up and forward, up and forward. She rewards him with an "Oh...oh...oh..." song like a triumphant melody of conquest, her body capturing pleasure from him even within the ropes.

Then his hand is gone, and the triumph becomes a frustrated whimper at the loss. He reaches up, hand still slick with juices, twisting his fingers in the soft, tiny tangles of her hair, pulling face down to cock, to take her mouth. But she is hungry for this, too, drawing him in, sucking and licking. She lets his cock pop out of her mouth for a moment and twists her head down, laving his balls, and now it is his mouth that opens, a wordless "Ahhhh..." escaping into the darkness at the sweet sensation.

His hand tightens again and he fucks her mouth hard, gagging her, taking her breath, but with every movement she pushes him, wanting more. She is devouring him, ignoring the reflexive rejection of her throat, pushing him deeper, thrusting, swallowing him down.

Feeling his orgasm already building, he roughly pushes her aside, letting her slump to the floor, hearing her chuckle. She knows how close she got him, and his come is a coup she longs to count. She can't see his face, but she knows he is grinning as fiercely as she as he grabs another rope and folds her leg in, pushing it double with the weight of his body. For a moment his hand lingers on the taut flexion of muscled ass that is exposed, fingers stroking a prelude to the ultimate goal. Then the rope winds tight across her thigh and shin, bound back again and again. This is not pretty decoration; this is rope for rough plea-sure, cinched tight with sure fingers that leave her tightly bound in the dark.

Another rope, another leg, this one tied as he crouches over her head, pressing his balls into her eager and welcoming mouth. She is bound but far from meek, and her powerful lust manifests in the furious stroke and suck of tongue and lips, drawing his balls full into her mouth, her tongue twisting circles round them.

Legs bound, he grabs the ropes on her arms, roughly pulling her to a kneeling position. She hisses as her body adjusts to the unfamiliar tension, baring her teeth in delightful and furious effort. The ropes twist and hold her body bent at the waist, and he lifts his cock again to her lips, reveling in the power of his grip in the soft crinkle of her hair matched by the driving intensity of her mouth as she goes down.

He pulls her up, kissing her violently, loving the taste of himself on her full lips, feeling the hot panting want of her breath close, their growls mingling as teeth nip at each other. He swivels on his knees around her body, a smooth predatory movement. She can feel his cock pressing along her cleft; the shaft feels perfect along the slick crevice. Instinctively, she pushes back against him, and his violent thrusting response burns her knees a few inches forward across the bedroom carpet.

She'll have those burns for weeks to come, matching his, but right now there is only the sweet impact of their bodies, feeling so good they both want more, harder, now. He thrusts again, pulling on her hair, her cry a sweet harmony of pain and desire and need. They are near the chair now, a barely seen outline in the dark, and with another sharp pull and thrust she is pressed against the seat, the edge digging into her upper chest with unyielding pressure that will leave her sore for days.

Not now, though. Now her mind and his are in this moment, filled with the urgencies of flesh and sex. He lets go of her hair, and she lays her head down on the soft cotton cushion. If there had been light, the expression of sweet contentment on her face might have baffled an observer. There is no witness but him, though, and his focus is elsewhere.

Her ass. Bound in this way, arms pulled hard behind her, legs buckled, he can lift her hips so she perches on her knees, presenting her taut, round cheeks in perfect and total accessibility. For the first time since the light left the room, he pauses, letting his fingertips run across her skin in the dark before rolling the condom down the solid length of his cock. She hums happily, giving a little wiggle of her hips in appreciation and anticipation. His hands grab her hips, bodies slick with sweat and spit and the slick juices of the battle of lust and will. There is a guttural sound coming from his chest as he drives his cock into her ass. There is no surrender here, no softness; while one is bound and one is naked, one thrusting and one penetrated, they are equal opponents and collaborators, his temporary advantage quickly met by the eager press of her asscheeks up to meet every slam of his hips.

This is primitive sex, and both of them move beyond thought, beyond even sensation, filled with the solid impact of their bodies moving together as he fucks her and she fucks him and it no longer matters, both of them taken by the simple urgency of pleasure taken from each other.

That is the moment. At some point they will come, or not. At some point they will clean up, open the window, drift into softer sleep with flaccid cock resting comfortably against the soft cotton of her panties. In some future, they will refer to this night again and her eyes will look up and to the left, remembering, and her smile at that moment will be the thing that he thinks of when he thinks of how much he loves her.

But that is later. More powerful than any of it is the moment, that one point held forever beyond the decay of memory. The moment of thrusting sweat, tight ropes and rough sex, stopping time and shrinking the world to two feral bodies, teeth bared in the dark.

IN HIS CONTROL

Jade Melisande

Juliette knelt at the feet of her lover, her head in his lap, her breathing finally beginning to slow. She curled her spine into the caress of his hand, enjoying the feel of his fingers lightly tracing the various welts, tender spots and already-forming bruises he found there.

"You did well today, Juli," he said, his voice as much a welcomed caress as his hand had been.

She smiled softly against his thigh. "Thank you, Sir." Pushing herself to go farther, to dig deeper into those physical places where fear and pain and euphoria collided and, eventually, intertwined, was a large part of the joy she experienced in what they did. And she had pushed herself hard today, hearing her safeword in her head over and over, but never uttering it. It was a personal challenge, one that she found profoundly satisfying. And she knew that he enjoyed taking her there as well, enjoyed knowing that she found such deep satisfaction in the physical side of what they did.

Besides, it made them both hot as hell.

He took her under the arms and lifted her compliant form up into his lap, where he cradled her for a moment before sitting her next to him on the couch. Sometimes their BDSM play culminated in sex, the kind that nearly tore them apart from the inside out with its intensity, sometimes it ended with her in a puddle on his lap. Cupping one hand under her chin, he looked into her eyes. "You did well," he said again, and stroked her cheek. "But I want more."

She blinked. She was exhausted. "More? I'm...I'm pretty well done in, Ian," she said uncertainly.

He shook his head. "I'm not talking about what we just did," he said. "I'm talking about in general. In our *relationship*." She tensed, and he paused for a moment, then continued when she stayed silent. "I've always wanted more, Juli. You know that. I want more than just your body. I want *this*." He tapped her lightly on the temple.

She shook her head, drawing away from him with her hands raised in an unconscious gesture, closing herself off before he had finished, already denying him in a way she never did physically. "That wasn't what we agreed to—"

He caught her hands, stilled her with his gaze. "I want to change the agreement."

"No," she said, "I can't. We can't—"

He pulled her to him and covered her mouth with his own. "We can do anything we want," he breathed against her mouth. "I want you, Juli. *All* of you." When she took a breath to protest further, he kissed her deeply.

"Give yourself to me, Juliette," he whispered, moving his lips from her mouth to her face, her neck, the place just behind her ear. His voice sent a shiver down her spine. He released one of her wrists and scooped his hand around the base of her neck and drew his lips down the delicate length of her throat and back up along the line of her jaw. Her head tipped back of its own accord, giving him greater access; her breath caught in her throat. The warmth of his mouth on her, tracing her flesh almost imperceptibly, sent shivers dancing across her skin. Her body felt electric, every touch almost painfully magnified.

"Be mine," he said. "Truly mine." It was not a plea, nor yet a demand; it was something in between, and she felt herself responding to it physically even as she struggled to keep her head. It was unfair, this assault on her senses when she was so vulnerable, so open, after the intensity of the session they had just shared.

"Please, Ian," she said, "don't ask this of me."

In answer he pushed her back against the pillows, recaptured both of her hands in one of his own and raised them above her head. Holding them captive, he stared down into her eyes as he followed the lines of her body with his free hand. He covered the fluttering pulse at her throat with a palm, making her take a sharp, startled breath, before moving his hand down to her shoulder, to press and caress the rope marks that still branded her skin. His eyes never leaving hers, he cupped her breast and tweaked her nipple, only recently liberated from clamps, making her jump and her breath whoosh out in a hiss. His eyes glittered at her reaction, a hint of a grin curving his lips. His hand skimmed over the indent at her waist to her softly curved and vulnerable belly, then opened over the flare of her hip and stroked across a smooth flank, where it lingered a moment on skin recently marked by his whip. She felt her cunt throb traitorously as he deliberately pressed his fingers into her tender flesh, and squirmed as he traced them lower, over the mound of her sex.

"Ian," she gasped, as he pushed a finger into her, and then another; he found her wet and open (as he had to have known she would be). When she writhed against him, he held her wrists tighter, leaning his whole body over her, pressing his weight into her in the way he knew she liked, as he finger-fucked her, slowly at first, and then with a brutal intensity that matched the ferocity of their earlier session. All the while he kept his eyes trained on hers, willing her to keep hers open as she moaned and strained toward her peak. She panted, pushing against him, fighting him even as she strained into him, striving to take all of him into her. And then her orgasm tore through her and she cried out, closing her eyes involuntarily, arching and bucking against him. When she had quieted once more, she opened her eyes to find his still on hers.

"Beautiful," he said, still not releasing her. "But it's not enough anymore." He shook his head slightly and sat back. "I love what we do, Juli, but..." He looked around, at her, at himself, at the space around them, encompassing all that their relationship was—and wasn't. "I can't do just...*this*...anymore."

Still struggling to control her breathing, Juli shook her head and felt her eyes filling with tears.

"I want more, Juli. More than just...the physical. Be *mine*, Juli. Give yourself—all of yourself—to me."

She took a shuddering breath. Saw everything that was between them in the heat and desire and love in his eyes. She reached a tentative hand out to touch him, stroked his chest, raised a hand to his face. She knew, in that moment, that she already *was* his.

"All right," she said. "Tell me what you want me to do."

Juliette stepped into the elevator of her apartment building and pressed the button to the garage. She glanced at the other passengers self-consciously, as though they could see what she wore beneath her clothes—what she *was*. Could the elderly woman from apartment three tell that something had changed in Juli? Could she tell that beneath her conservative gray suit, Juli wore under things Ian had picked out for her, under things completely inappropriate for the office? Could the building super tell that she had made agreements with Ian that she never had with anyone else, giving him control over her life in small but significant ways? She fidgeted a bit as the car made its slow progress to the ground, then escaped her neighbors' (knowing?) looks gratefully as soon as the door sprang open.

Once inside her car, she pulled out her phone and texted Ian. He had emailed her that morning with instructions regarding her clothing, what she could eat and drink throughout the day, and he had told her to text him when she was on her way to work.

"Little things first, Juli," he'd said. "Small things that will hardly matter in the larger scheme of things, but that will remind you of me and the commitment that we have made to each other throughout the day. Your clothing, your food, your drinks. And one other thing." But he wouldn't tell her what that other thing was, no matter how she had entreated him. "This is what giving up control is, Juli. Do you trust me? Do you truly trust that I wouldn't ask anything of you that would be too hard, that would harm you?"

"Yes, of course," she had responded immediately. And she did. It wasn't fear of harm that made her anxious, it was…loss of control. It was that it was something that *he* chose. "I'll tell you in the morning," was all he would say.

Good girl, he texted back. *Now this is what I want from you…*

She couldn't stop thinking about it. As soon as she'd read his instructions, she'd felt her body clench, felt the need to urinate. That was what his last instruction was: that she ask permission to pee. She stepped into her office building and shuddered delicately. It wasn't just that it was embarrassing; it was the point of the thing! She had some small amount of pride. Would he take that away from her? She hadn't liked it, but she had agreed to let him choose her clothing, food and drinks. But to have to call or text to use the bathroom—that was too much. In fact, she thought, she'd end this right now...

She put her purse down in the cubicle she shared with the other executive assistant and headed to the bathroom. But once inside she stopped cold and stared at the stall door, biting her lip. Was this how it would end, then, with her unable to do this one small thing he had asked of her?

Hannah, the other assistant, walked in behind her, hitting the door against her as she did. "Oh! I'm sorry, Juliette. I didn't see you standing there. What are you looking at? Are the toilets backing up again?"

"No," she said, "I..." But what could she say? *I'm just thinking about disobeying my lover by peeing without permission?* "I thought I saw a spider," she finished lamely. And then, because it would be odd not to, she went into the stall. She realized, even as she did, that she wasn't going to use the toilet. But she pulled up her skirt and slid the sheer silk panties down her thighs, because that was what one did in the bathroom. A wave of pure eroticism passed through her as she did so. She was wearing these panties, the stockings and garter belt not just *for* Ian, as she had done to entice him in the past, but because *he had told her to do so.* She skimmed a hand along the silk of her stockings, enjoying the pure sensuous pleasure of them against her skin. She imagined Ian's hands sliding over them as she hovered over the toilet and she felt an unexpected throb between her legs. Then she had to fight her body's natural urge to urinate, now that she was in the customary position. Her body didn't know that her mind had changed the rules. Unless she really did intend to disobey—

No, she wouldn't disobey. The effort of stopping herself, the clenching of muscles to still the impending flow of liquid, gave her another unexpected jolt of erotic pleasure. She took a deep, shaky breath and her hand trembled as she pulled her panties back up. Unable to stop herself, she slid a finger over the cool silk, pressing it against the heat of her cunt and feeling it get wet as she did. She bit back a moan and stroked her fingers lightly over her clit. She thought about Ian's fingers in her the night she'd submitted to his demands and felt a shock of heat race through her, centering on the throb between her legs. She realized suddenly that she was so aroused it would only take moments for her to come, right there in the employee restroom.

She snatched her hand away from herself and struggled to control her breathing and calm her wildly throbbing arousal. That, too, was now in Ian's control.

Trembling, but schooling herself back into "executive assistant" mode, she turned and automatically flushed the empty toilet. When she stepped out to wash her hands, equally automatically, Hannah was there, at the sink. She met Juli's eyes in the mirror. Juli imagined she could smell the musky scent of her arousal, see the flush that she knew was spreading over her chest. But Hannah merely smiled and held open the bathroom door for her.

At her desk, Juliette resumed her morning's routine, trying to keep her mind on things other than the restroom and Ian's instructions. Twice she got up to relieve herself and be damned with the game; twice she sat back down. Each time it was as though her world narrowed down to that space between her legs, and she realized she was getting wetter every time she thought about it. Hannah glanced over the top of her computer at her curiously the second time.

"You're fidgety this morning, Juli," she said.

Juli felt the flush climbing up her chest to her neck. "I...I guess I had too much coffee this morning," she said. At least that much was true. Ian had allowed her a large latte that morning. Too late she'd realized that he might have had an ulterior motive in encouraging her to drink that much fluid.

At a quarter to ten, her boss came sauntering into the office. He frequently came in late and left early, but woe to her if she ever called in sick. And if he came in late and left early, she was the opposite, oftentimes having to cancel plans to finish some last-minute project that he just *had* to get done for the following morning, but which he hadn't given her adequate notice to complete by the end of the regular work day. She didn't know why she put up with it, and in fact Ian had told her more than once that she ought not to. She had the experience and skills to go anywhere, if she'd just work up the courage to *do* so.

"Juliette," her boss said now, as he passed her desk, "I have a project that needs to get done today. Can you come into my office?"

As Juliette gathered her notepad and pen, she saw Hannah roll her eyes and shake her head. "Hope you didn't have plans tonight," she mouthed. Juliette grimaced and got up to follow her boss.

As she stood, she felt the slide of silk between her thighs and imagined it made a soft whisper against her skin. Her bladder felt full, distended against her pubis; every step was an exquisite ache. She thought of Ian and his hands on her; thought of how pleased he would be that she had obeyed him. *If* she obeyed him. She still hadn't made up her mind to give in and text him.

Ten minutes later she was back at her desk, fuming. There

was no way she was going to be able to finish the report that her boss needed "first thing" the next morning by the end of the workday. She'd be lucky to be able to finish it by seven—and she *did* have plans. The worst part of it was that she hadn't said a word. She'd just taken notes, nodded her head, and left his office. Hannah looked at her pityingly as she settled back at her desk. Maybe if she worked through lunch she could leave in time and not have to change her plans. Juli thought about the countless job offers she had turned down during her eighteen months at the firm and wondered why she'd never had the nerve to even entertain the idea of leaving. How could she be so resistant to submitting to Ian's control, to submitting to a man she trusted and loved, and yet be so willing to accept her boss's tyranny?

The next hour was exquisite torture. Soon all she could think about was the need to pee. Every time she thought about it, she had to clench her thighs together, and soon she felt the juncture between her legs growing steadily slicker with moisture that had nothing to do with urine. She actually had to suppress a moan at one point as she found herself drifting from the report she was writing to thoughts of Ian and his hands on her, his mouth against hers, his words in her ear. "Give yourself to me, Juli..." Why was this one thing so, so hard for her to do? She knew he would be pleased when she texted him, asking permission. She knew that he knew how hard this was for her.

But still she resisted.

As though he'd heard her thoughts, her phone flashed with a text message from Ian. Her chest grew tight and heat washed over her as she picked up her phone and opened the message.

I'm surprised I haven't heard from you, it said. *You must be...uncomfortable by now.*

She *was* uncomfortable. Just reading his words intensified

the urge to relieve herself. Guilt flashed through her. Why was she resisting this so hard? Was it pure stubbornness...or something else?

I'm fine, she replied back, though she felt anything but fine. *Boss is giving me grief.*

I'm the only one allowed to give you grief, he said. She smiled at his words, imagining the grin behind them, but a moment later she caught her breath as his next message flashed on the screen.

I know you can do this, Juli, it read. *Don't be afraid.*

And just like that, she realized that was what had been holding her back. Fear. Fear of letting go, of truly giving him control.

Her phone intercom buzzed. "Do you have the Cox report finished?" her boss barked.

She glanced at the report folder lying on her desk. She had put it aside to work on the new project he'd given her. "No," she said, "I've been working on the one you gave me this morning—"

"You can work on that after you get the Cox report to me," he said, interrupting her.

"But Mr. Garreth, I won't be able to finish the new one before I leave if—"

"Juliette," he interrupted again, his voice sharp with censure, "I really didn't expect finishing your work on time to be such a difficulty for you. You've never had this issue before."

Because she'd never objected to working until seven before!

She took a deep breath and felt the fullness of her bladder, the incredible need to let go. And more than that. She sat there, contemplating her morning, her resistance to Ian's instructions—and her acquiescence to this tyrannical man who meant nothing to her. Cradling the phone between her shoulder and ear, she picked up her cell phone and looked at Ian's last message. And suddenly, she wasn't afraid anymore. Of herself or her boss.

Please, Sir, she typed, *may I go pee?* Her hand didn't even shake as she hit send. She returned her attention to her boss.

"I can't do that, Mr. Garreth," she said firmly, interrupting him mid-rant.

"Excuse me?" His voice sounded thoroughly shocked. She had never, ever interrupted him. Or told him no.

"I won't be able to finish that report for you tonight." She eyed her phone as it lit up with a text from Ian. As she read it, her body responded automatically, as though it knew who owned it. And as she felt the warmth flowing from her body onto the seat beneath her, she smiled. "I'll be looking for another job," she said.

PAPER DOLL

joy

The dress was, in a word, scandalous. Hope had never worn anything so revealing in her life, a little black number made completely of lace. It hit her thigh dangerously close to her sex and had an embarrassing tendency to ride up, revealing her beautifully rounded ass.

The day before, Matthew had pulled ten crisp twenty-dollar bills from his leather wallet, pressing them into her waiting palm with a grin. "You may buy anything you like, my beauty," he'd told Hope quietly, his expression free of emotion save the familiar glint in his dark eyes. "But there are a few provisions. Nothing below your knees. At least one piece of lingerie. One pair of shoes, and something made of leather."

"Yes, Sir," she'd replied. Hope had thought he was done giving his instructions and gave him a reluctant smile, lifting herself from his white leather couch and stuffing the brand-new bills into her jeans pocket. She could have sworn she saw Matthew cringe as the crisp bills were crumpled and wrinkled beneath her fingers. He had such an eye for beauty that he could not stand to see something that had been perfect suddenly ruined with carelessness. Hope hid an amused grin and slung her purse over her shoulder, leaning upward on her toes to kiss him. Matthew returned the kiss cordially before breaking it and holding one finger up to her, then playfully turning to press it on the tip of her nose.

"And I want something see-through."

The party was almost over, and Hope sat in the chair with her selections, tallying up prices to make sure that she had enough money to cover the cost. Mistress Katrina was a professional dominatrix who often used her in-home dungeon as a venue to promote her other business: fetish wear. A stunning woman, it was no surprise that men would pay Katrina to feed their dirty little obsessions. Her curves were dangerous, her eyes piercing blue, her hair fiery red. The woman dripped of sex. She'd gone into fetish wear as a side business, she once told Hope, because she wanted all women to see how truly beautiful they were capable of being. Hope secretly doubted that any clothing could make her feel "truly beautiful."

Mistress Katrina's parties were always special occasions because it was rare that you would have immediate access to such a wide range of fetish clothing. Normally, you had to go online to buy them, wait weeks for them to come in the mail, and hope to god that they fit. Matthew was ecstatic that Mistress Katrina was holding another one of her special parties, but Hope was less enthusiastic about the whole endeavor.

She wasn't at all used to wearing anything sexy. Actually, up until about six months ago, it had been extremely rare for her to wear anything above her knees. She was afraid of her own body and had been for most of her life. Matthew had tried to slowly help her overcome her self-consciousness. He would spend countless time, money and energy in pursuit of his slave's self-confidence, buying her everything from curve-hugging leather dresses with zip-up vests that showed off her breasts, to casual denim skirts that emphasized her perfect ass and legs. She was appalled at it, but what could she do? He wanted other people's eyes on her. And Matthew always got what he wanted.

Who she had been no longer existed with Matthew; Hope the small-town girl next door, Hope the good little Baptist, Hope the golden child had all become Hope the slut. Part of her was horrified, but another, stronger part of her relished the feeling. Her newfound identity was freeing. She no longer had to be any of those things into which her upbringing had trapped her. She was free to be who she was and not what society expected her to be. She no longer had to worry that "good girls don't want this" or that "good girls don't do that." Fuck what good girls do and what good girls want. She wasn't a good girl. Not with him. He gave her permission not to be that way. He preferred her not to be. He demanded that she not be.

Hope stood in front of the full-length mirror in the back of Mistress Katrina's dungeon, hands running along the lace of the shocking dress. Mistress Katrina's lips had curled into a salacious grin, and she clapped her gloved hands together like an excited child. "Oh, Matthew would never forgive me if I let you walk out of here without this dress!" *And I want something see-through*, Matthew's voice echoed in Hope's mind. This certainly did fit the bill.

What a rich, wonderful thing it was to know that Matthew was proud of her and that she had pleased him, simply by being who she was. Hope sat silently on her black fur mat at his feet, hugging her knees tightly to her breasts, her eyes closed in

sensual bliss. He was brushing her hair tenderly, her favorite
music playing softly in the background.

"Sir?" she inquired of him as he lovingly groomed her.

"Yes?"

"Have you always taken such good care of all your girls?" He
smiled softly, turning her to face him. His hand gently brushed
a dark tendril back from her face, his thumb stroking her cheek
affectionately.

"No."

Something see-through...

His voice echoed in her mind as she stood in front of the
full-length mirror that hung in his hallway, her hands running
along the lace of the shocking dress. He'd instructed her to wear
it. He'd allowed her no pasties, not even a thong or nylons. The
only covering on her body was the see-through lace and a pair
of strappy black heels. Self-consciously, Hope studied her own
awkward reflection. The outfit covered nothing. The hem of the
skirt stopped just below the curve of her ass, and the neckline
stopped just above her burgundy nipples; they stuck out through
the holes in the delicate lace when they were hard. Hope bit her
bottom lip hard, catching it between her teeth and chewing on
it, staring at herself in the mirror as she practiced positions that
might serve to hide her imperfections. A hand here would hide
her tummy. Standing at the right angle would make her ass look
smaller. Perhaps if she put one leg directly in front of the other,
she'd create the illusion of being skinnier all around. But there
was just no way to hide. Not in this thing. Hope may as well
have been naked.

Hearing Matthew's voice from the living room, she moved
quickly from the bathroom and down the hallway, stopping
in the archway to his living room and playfully turning as she

had seen models do on television, laughing aloud as she did. He grinned. That boyish grin alarmed her. His footsteps were deliberate as he moved toward her, his hand running lightly along her spine before his fingers found refuge in the thick dark hair at the nape of her neck. He curled them into a fist and pulled firmly, leaning forward to let his lips brush against her ear. His dark eyes met hers in the mirror, holding her captive in his gaze.

"Go to my room. Wait for me there. Keep the light off and listen to the radio. Do. Not. Move."

"Yes, Sir."

Back down the hall she went, hips swaying seductively as he had taught her, concentrating on the soft *click-click* of her heels on the hardwood floor, eyes lifted only momentarily to a painting of a woman on a throne that hung at the end of the hallway. She looked much like Mistress Katrina, and the slave beneath her was curled up so that one leg was crossed over the other, her full breasts resting on either side of her knee, a chain dangling teasingly between her nipples. *I wish I looked like that.* The thought ran through Hope's mind before she could stop it. She sighed and gave a disapproving shake of her head at the painting before slipping slowly into the dark room; Hope stumbled about clumsily until she found the bed. She slowly lowered herself onto it, hands on her lap, chewing nervously on her lower lip. It was a bad habit that she still had not managed to break.

She was counting the number of songs as she sat silently. Three. Four. Five. Still, she was left sitting there in his room, pulling at the hem of her dress. She strained to try to hear what he was doing, but she could hear nothing. Her stomach was nervous, her heart pounding loudly in her ears.

Finally, the silhouette of Matthew's handsome form appeared in the doorway. Hope let her eyes glance over the outline of his well-built frame, her tongue sliding across her lips. She still could not understand why he would choose her. She was not the most attractive of women. If you asked her, she was awkward looking. Her butt was too big, her breasts too small and she had entirely too much weight on her hips. Matthew, though, always gazed upon her as though she were some work of art. Perhaps to him, she was. A work of art that he had sculpted. She slowly stood, smiling nervously at him, but he only extended his hand and silently led her to the door. The jingling of keys in his hand caused her to pause and lift her green eyes to him, feet stopping a few paces from the doorway.

"Where are we going?" she blurted. The question seemed to pop out of her mouth of its own accord.

"I didn't tell you, did I?"

"No, Sir..."

"Then don't ask." There was a sharp blow delivered to her backside that made her yelp in pain. Hope's mouth went dry, and she was afraid at first that she'd gotten herself into trouble...but when he'd turned his back to her again, Hope was sure she detected a slight curve of his lips and a low chuckle deep in his throat.

His truck was always difficult to get into, especially in heels. In a dress this short, it was impossible to get into the vehicle in anything resembling a ladylike fashion. She had to flash something. Her Master was watching in thinly veiled amusement as Hope climbed in, causing her dress to ride up almost to her waist. She began to nervously fidget with it, acutely aware of exactly where the hem had landed.

"Leave it." His voice was firm and commanding. His very tone turned her on almost instantly, her nipples sticking out

through the lacy fabric. He gave them each a tweak and closed
the door. She found she actually had to sit on her hands to keep
from pulling her dress down to where she thought it needed to
be. As much as he had made it clear that he adored the curves of
her body, Hope always thought she could have stood to have a
few less curves. And she certainly didn't want them on display.

The drive was silent and painful. *Where the hell was he
going?* The thoughts rushed through her head, and Hope was
completely unable to stop them. She felt hot tears begin to sting
her eyes as she saw him driving farther and farther into the
city. Her imagination was out of control. He could be going
anywhere—a restaurant, a bar, a club...oh, god, what if she ran
into someone she knew? What if she was caught by her employer
or her family, being paraded about practically naked? What if
Matthew's boss saw them?

"Sir?" she began meekly. He didn't even look in her direction. Hope tried again, a little louder this time, fingertips digging
hard into her thighs, her nails leaving little half-moons in her
flesh. "Sir?" She spoke a little louder, with a little more enthusiasm. Still he didn't look up. Unable to contain her panic any
longer, she gasped for air, reaching out to curl her small fingers
around his arm. "Matthew! I can't do this...turn the car around
and take me home. I mean it...I don't want to play. Just take me
home. Please."

Painful silence filled the truck for a few moments as Hope sat
there with a vise grip on his arm, his eyes never leaving the road.
After what seemed like ages, the truck stopped at a stoplight and
Matthew turned sideways in the seat, his large hand reaching
out to take Hope gently but firmly by the jaw, forcing her to
look into his eyes. His words were filled with quiet resolve.

"It pleases me. And you will do what pleases me."

"But, Sir..."

"Shh." He hushed her and affectionately brushed a tear from her cheek before pulling away from the stoplight. "It pleases me."

It pleases me. And Matthew's pleasure was all that mattered. Hope turned to face front again. Her tear-filled eyes made all the lights of the city blurry, traffic lights and signs and head-lights blending together in a misty collage. She could make out a green billboard with white lettering, flashing neon signs advertising exotic dancers, a brightly decorated limousine with flowers, painted windows, and old cans dragging along behind it. Feeling sick to her stomach, Hope closed her eyes tightly, forcing the tears from them to spill onto her cheeks. Earlier that evening, he'd been so tender. So affectionate. Matthew had never told Hope that he loved her. It wasn't in him to say such things, but the little things he did told her as much. Through his actions, he constantly told her what she already knew. He treasured her. He loved her. He would care for her. She was safe.

The car was parked when she finally snapped awake from her daydream, and she was watching as Matthew moved to the other side of the truck. He opened the door for her and took her hand to help her down out of the car. With a simple gesture, he ordered her to lace her fingers behind her neck, turning her around and pulling her dress down so that the hem hit her midthigh. She no longer protested. The length of the hem didn't matter. The lace material of the dress could cover up none of her body. She was naked, and he was going to parade her about. She supposed she could take it as a high compliment, if she could get past the paralyzing fear she still felt rising up within her.

Matthew turned her back around, letting his hands wander about her body. Hope was sure, from the way he chuckled, that he could feel how hard and fast her heart was pounding. He leaned down, his hands wrapping around her waist and whispering softly into her ear. "You are so beautiful, my girl. I'm sure everyone will think so."

His hands grasped her own, guiding them back down to her sides. Attention turned to protocol and made it easier to put service at the forefront of her mind. When she concentrated on his pleasure more than her own irrational fears, it became less difficult. She walked to his left side, exactly three paces behind him. When he was training her, he'd insisted on hearing two distinct sounds when she walked in heels. His rules also demanded that her eyes remain focused only on his feet. This was convenient for him; it meant that she would not be able to see the building they were walking into. He held the door open for Hope, who stepped through the threshold shakily, then waited as he again took his place in front of her.

Her heels were immediately silenced on the carpeted floor of the store. The bad lighting and cheesy music one often thinks of in a porn shop was missing from this establishment, which was surprisingly classy and inviting. As she moved inside with her Master, she instantly felt eyes all over her. She stopped, all at once feeling unable to continue. He turned to her. Somehow he always knew what she was thinking. His eyes were gleaming with pride, a smile playing on his lips.

"Yes," he said, "you can."

The three words were all the encouragement she needed. After all, if Matthew said that she could do something, if her Master believed she was able, who was she to argue with him? He knew his possession well enough to know what her abilities were. *Yes, I can.*

She saw him nod to the young man sitting behind the counter, but she was more keenly aware of the way this man was openly staring at her. She wasn't used to this open kind of appraisal, and she shifted her weight awkwardly from one foot to the other, fingers pulling at the hem of her dress. It clung to her body in an odd sort of way that she found both sexy and annoying. Matthew had been talking to the guy behind the counter regarding a certain little toy he had wanted for her, but the conversation was temporarily put on hold when he turned to her, a disapproving look on his face as he observed her nervous fidgeting.

"Hands behind you," he barked at her suddenly, the sharpness of his voice jerking her violently from her thoughts. "Legs apart. Now! Farther. Yes, good girl. Stay. You are not to move."

Matthew turned back to the man, who now had one arm leaning on the counter. From his elbow to his wrist, black ink decorated his skin. Hope squinted, leaning forward so she could inspect the tattoo. It was a cross, decorated with flowers and draped in cloth. Interwoven in the flowers were three words: No MORE PAIN.

Turning from the man, Hope's attention moved to the decorations. Reproductions of Impressionist paintings decorated all of the walls. It seemed a little incongruous to her. Monet's *Water Lilies* was hanging right above a small shelf full of flavored condoms. And what of *Clair de Lune* as an accompaniment to the buzzing of vibrators as they were tested at the register? Finding it all a bit too odd to dwell on, she turned her gaze once again to the patrons. Unable to look into their faces, Hope focused on their shoes wandering silently about on the pillowy, off-white carpet. Most of them were polished to a high shine, the crease of perfectly pressed slacks lying atop their toes. Every last one was wearing a business suit, and every last one of them was staring straight at her.

All of her energy was being poured into the uncomfortable

stillness Master had commanded of her. She hated him at that moment as he made her stand in the center of a building, men all around her, gawking at her as if she were an object. Tears were stinging her eyes as she looked at Master again in desperation, pleading silently with him to get her out of here. *Just take me home*, she begged inwardly. Her arousal, though, was unmistakable. Her nipples peeked through the lace fabric invitingly. One gentleman with bright blue eyes and cross-shaped cufflinks on his sleeves looked down at them, then winked at her with a grin. Her face was flushed a deep red, her heart pounding so loud in her ears that she couldn't hear herself think. Hope felt trapped. She was unable to look anywhere without being blatantly reminded of the situation. She saw the man behind the desk looking her up and down again, slowly.

Suddenly, the feeling of humiliation and objectification, while it didn't go away, wasn't so bad anymore. These men told no lies and sugarcoated nothing. There was only honesty in their enjoyment of the beauty of her body, and the shamelessness of lust and desire. It was a refreshing and honest way of looking at someone, free of games, free of fear. It turned her on in a way she couldn't explain. She felt her juices moistening her inner thighs, and she was sure that the musky scent could be smelled throughout the entire building. The suspicion was confirmed as Matthew turned and grinned at her. There it was again, that boyish smile that appeared when he knew that his will was being exalted above hers. He took her by the hand and led her down the aisle. Her full hips continued to sway from side to side, and the seductive manner in which she moved only served to draw more attention to herself. She felt at least a dozen pairs of eyes drilling into the back of her head like lasers.

Hope was amazed. She was actually doing this—because it pleased him. Her preferences were not an option. Matthew wanted; Hope gave. That was how this worked. It didn't matter whether she liked it.

In the midst of that shop, with all those people watching her, Hope's mind took her back to her very first party. She'd been so frightened. The same sick feeling in the pit of her stomach that she'd suffered in the truck was present at that party. She'd been led up onto a large stage and tied securely to a cross in front of a hundred people, stripped down to a thong and pasties, then teased, flogged and humiliated. It brought her to a place in her own mind that she neither understood nor wanted to understand. She just wanted to feel. It was scary as hell, and that made it hotter still. That night, he'd taken a pair of safety scissors and cut the clothing from her body, shred by shred. The way the air suddenly attacked her flesh, Matthew's fingertips running up and down her legs and back and leaving goose bumps in their wake...Hope remembered every single sensation as though it was still happening. More than anything, she remembered the feeling of shock and panic when he leaned his body up against hers, her bare breasts pressing into the cold of the wooden frame's finish. His hands crept along her arms, from shoulders to wrists, his breath hot in her ear as he whispered to her.

"Everyone's watching you..."

She was trembling. She didn't know whether it was from fear or the rush of endorphins...or maybe both. She didn't know whether to laugh or cry, and as a result she appeared to be in shock. He led her back to the truck, the bag that held his purchase clutched tightly in Hope's hands. He turned her toward him before helping her into the car, his fingers tenderly caressing her flushed, burning cheeks. Suddenly, Matthew grabbed her shoulders, forcefully pulling her body tightly up against his own. He kissed her roughly and hungrily before stepping back, his hands over her nearly nude form as he admired her.

"My god, you are beautiful," he crooned into her ear. A smile spread across her face, pleasure welling up from deep within her.

"So you are proud of me, Sir?" She looked up at him, joy filling her eyes. He lifted a hand to brush a dark tendril from her eyes, just as he had done earlier that evening. Leaning forward, Matthew let his breath push the words past his lips, that ever-present spark in his eye. "You belong to me. You are my possession. What's not to be proud of?"

SUBBING

Rachel Kramer Bussel

It's just for a day," Jesse wheedled, begging her best friend, Taylor, to fill in for her on the job. "And you're already kinky," she added, like that sealed the deal, like Taylor would want to spend her Saturday bending over to get spanked and pretending to drool over some guy she wasn't interested in. It was true, she was kinky, not to mention single, but even though they were best friends, Jesse didn't know everything that Taylor was into. She didn't know how much Taylor had loved it when her ex, Brian, choked her, his big meaty hand wrapped around her slender neck while one leg pinned her down and his fingers pressed deep inside her. Jesse definitely didn't know how much Taylor liked it when Brian had called her a slut and "threatened" to bring his friends over to fill all her holes and cover her in come. The dirtier the talk, the harder she'd come. But that was with Brian, not some stranger, even though, she had to admit, when Brian had teased her with the idea of being his whore, getting paid to service his friends, she'd practically crushed the fingers he'd been fucking her with.

In the end, it wasn't the excitement that made Taylor say yes, but the fact that, even more than she was a bad girl, she was a good girl. She knew Jesse would've done anything for her, and she couldn't refuse this rare favor. If she'd fill in for a friend working a cash register or serving as a teaching assistant, her other closest friends' current jobs, she couldn't refuse to get fucked for cash. Well, not fucked, Jesse clarified. "No sex," she said, either ignoring or not seeing Taylor's slight slump of disappointment. Wasn't getting fucked the best part, the icing on the kinky cake?

"Okay, you just let them order you around, spank you, tie you up, stuff like that. Some of them want to see you do things to yourself, like suck your own nipple or put a butt plug in. But they can't take photos of you and they can only touch you if you let them. You get a flat fee and you get to keep whatever tips they give you. And dinner wherever you want is on me."

"What should I wear?" Taylor asked. Fashion first was always her motto.

Jesse laughed. "Whatever you want. They're probably going to want you naked anyway. Some of them bring in clothes for you to try on. It's a job, Taylor; you don't have to love it, you just have to pretend to." Jesse gave her all the details, along with a hug and a smile, and left Taylor alone. The obliging friend plopped down in front of her TV, but all she could think about was the fact that tomorrow at this time, she could be doing anything, with anyone. Well, not anything, but almost; the thought made her wet, and before she knew it, the TV was off and her electric vibrator was in her hand, making her come as she envisioned two men toying with her, one pressing her down onto her knees to suck the other's cock while he beat her with a riding crop. She knew as her orgasm hit she wouldn't have to fake anything; even a guy she wasn't into was a guy paying for her services, paying for her to show him what a slut she really was. She would be subbing, but she wouldn't be acting, she didn't think.

Taylor showed up for the gig in what she thought was appropriate attire: a simple yet relatively see-through white T-shirt, her nipples jutting forward just enough to make it clear she didn't have on a bra, and a pleated black and red schoolgirl skirt, along with knee-high white socks and shiny black loafers she'd borrowed from her roommate. When in doubt, go for the schoolgirl look, she'd figured. She'd debated until the very last minute—panties or no panties—but had decided on plain white cotton; she could always take them off. She'd packed a toy bag just in case the dungeon didn't have exactly what her clients requested, although how she could predict what they'd want, she wasn't sure.

"Hello," she told the woman at the dungeon's front desk, who explained that most of the women working there were dommes, and most of their clients usually filled the role she was going to play today. Some of the men were switches, but the ones who mainly wanted a professional sub, which cost more, were usually rich and had limited time on their hands to find a girl willing to do the things he wanted them to do. Plus there were plenty of civilian women who actually wanted to get spanked and strung up, so the rich types didn't have to look too far for girls willing to take orders. The ones who wanted to pay for it had a reason and usually wanted something beyond the average kinky girl's regular repertoire, and Taylor was grateful for that, since she didn't consider herself an "average" anything. She read over the rules, which mentioned the company safeword that all clients were required to agree to, and waited, wondering if it was a faux pas, a mark of an amateur, that she was wet as could be. She was definitely glad she'd worn the panties.

She spied the men coming in, but couldn't discern a pattern. Most were at least in their thirties, many in their fifties, mostly white. Some were hot and hunky, but most were average; it was like a Wall Street parade, no hint of the business about to happen inside from these men's attire. And then she was called on. "Tina," said the clerk, using the name she'd picked, a simple one she would surely remember, one she was sometimes called by vague acquaintances who saw her rarely and couldn't quite recall her more manly moniker. She smiled to herself, knowing that if Jesse hadn't asked her to sub as a sub, she'd be sitting at her favorite coffee shop right now, hunched over some tedious manuscript she was copyediting. This was sure to be far more fun, not to mention lucrative.

She entered the room and wondered where to sit: on one of the chairs? On the floor? Should she stand? They said that the sub was truly the one in control of any kinky scene, but she wasn't so sure about that. Suddenly Taylor had butterflies in her stomach; she wanted to do a good job, on principle, and she wanted it to hurt, in a good way. She needed that rush of endorphins that only submission could give her, and as she took a deep breath in through her nose and slowly let it out through her mouth, she smiled to herself. Yes, she was woman enough to own that she wanted this, that she wasn't really in a chilly dungeon for the money, but for the rush, the thrill, the wetness. She was there because whether cash was involved or not, this was where she belonged.

Taylor decided to kneel, and kept her hands behind her back as she waited for the door to open. She'd been given a buzzer she could press to get security if she needed it, but when the door opened and an older man, one surely at least twice her own twenty-four years, entered, she knew she wasn't going to need it. He wasn't her usual type; he was a little more distinguished yet country, no hint of hipster about him; his aura was stern without trying. There was something old-fashioned about him, like he would be as happy handling a worn leather belt as he might using an implement found in one of her favorite sex toy stores. This man could beat her all over and she'd probably just ask for more. The trick, she'd learned early on, was in holding off on letting them know just how much you liked it. That wouldn't be hard, because Taylor—*Tina*, she reminded herself—liked struggling, even if it meant the internal struggling of keeping her deepest fantasies hidden.

"Hello, Tina, sweetheart," he said, his smile both sweet and sadistic at once. She glanced immediately at his crotch, a bad habit she'd picked up somewhere along the way with guys she was hot for. She could see the outline of his cock against his jeans. "Daddy wants to have a word with you." He took the chair and ragged it across the room, resting his hand on his cock. She looked up at him, grateful he wasn't overly polite, wasn't polluting their time with niceties that would do nothing for her pussy. He knew what he wanted, and so did she. "I have your allowance right here," he said, holding up what she could see was at least a hundred dollars more than her fee. "Crawl to me, pretty girl," he said. "Crawl to Daddy." She did, wondering if he could tell how wet she was, wondering if he knew this was her first time, wondering if any of that mattered.

He kept talking as she reached him, seamlessly sliding the bills into the waistband of her skirt. "I know it was really Janet who stole the car, but since you told me you did it, you're going to get punished for it. You understand, don't you?" Somehow, his voice was soothing, deep and sexy, like he was trying to seduce her, yet the power behind his words vibrated through the air. "Janet will get punished even worse," he said, "but you need to learn not to cover for her. You never lie to your Daddy again, do you hear me?" He didn't yell, but it was the quiet roar in his voice that cued her in. She knew she could back away if she wanted to, but she had no desire to escape; instead, she was irresistibly drawn to that cruel yet sweet voice, its roughness promising pain as well as tender understanding. "Now get me my whip," he said, pointing to a riding crop sticking up out of his briefcase. "Bring it to me between those pretty lips."

She shuddered as she did it, realizing it had been three months since she'd last been beaten, and two more since she'd had someone talk to her like this. Well, not like this, exactly; she'd only played at being a "bad girl," but never Daddy's bad girl. This was different, doubly, even triply hot for all the taboos they were breaking. "You're to keep your panties on, but I want you to show me how wet you are, Tina, show me how much you need to be punished." She pulled down her panties and bent over with the crop between her teeth, her ass in the air. Taylor spread her legs just enough to show the stranger, her new insta-Daddy, how slick her sex was. She started to inch backward, and stopped. Her punishment wasn't going to be a beating there, nor would there be a reward of his fingers or tongue or cock, as she was used to. Her real punishment was that she'd have to wait until later to touch herself there, where she most wanted it.

"I'm going to have to punish you even more for looking so good and teasing your old man, aren't I?" he asked, almost to himself, as he turned her around and grabbed the crop. He stood then used the crop to push her against the wall. "Hands up," he said, and she reached above her, holding on to the metal hooks fitted just for girls like her. He lifted her T-shirt and shoved it between her lips. "Keep that there or I'll rip it off; I bought it for you for your birthday, so technically it's mine—just like you are," he said.

She was aching, dripping, frantic before the crop even touched her. The first touch wasn't a strike but a tease, as it brushed against her hard right nipple like a feather would, except this feather was made of leather, and she knew it wasn't always going to feel so gentle. The man ran the crop all along her front, under each breast, along her gently sloping belly, up her neck. He let it rest gently against her cheek and meandered it along her underarm until she almost sighed in frustration. It was *on*; he tapped it against one nipple then hit the other one. Each nipple rose to attention, and after only a few slaps of the crop, Taylor was gritting her teeth, torn between watching the leather tip strike her tender nubs and closing her eyes to try to deal with the pain, the heat, the glorious rush she got each time the toy landed on her.

Just when her nipples felt like they were on fire, the man once again moved the crop down her body, this time to her inner thighs. He lifted her skirt and nudged her legs apart with his knee, then whapped her inner thighs. Taylor clutched the metal tightly, lest she sink down to the ground or be tempted to grab the crop and rub it against her wetness. The tender, padded flesh leading up to her sex had never been given quite so much attention, and Taylor bit her lip, aching with the sharp, pointed heat he managed to convey so expertly, like he was born to beat girls like her. She could almost forget they were actually playing a game, one in which she got paid for this, and simply be a girl who liked pain, craved it, needed it. It wasn't until that exact moment that Taylor—as Tina—fully owned her innate submissiveness, her masochism that made even the hint of pain, like when the head of the crop teased her by merely resting against her skin, cause her to feel like she wanted to writhe in ecstasy.

Taylor mashed her lips together, suddenly longing for something between them, something to suck on or simply fill her
up, and the look she gave the stranger was one of pure desire,
one she was sure he could read just as clearly as the tears that
sprouted to her eyes when he let the crop dangle and brushed
a thumb lightly over her trembling lower lip. He moved closer,
pressing her tight to the wall for a few seconds, then withdrew
and raised his hand to her cheek. She shuddered so hard she
thought she might come. "There's so much I'd love to do to you,
sweet girl," he said softly, an equally fervent need crashing right
through his voice. Taylor knew they were sharing a moment,
a real one, despite its trappings, and her pussy actually hurt
as it clenched around nothing. He'd landed one slap across her
tender face and brushed away the tear that trickled down, when
a buzzer sounded, signaling they only had five minutes left.
Taylor twitched, wondering if the sub could request more time.

Get a hold of yourself, she thought. *This is a job, a favor,
not your life. But it is*, another voice inside her said. Not this
dungeon, but this—the pain, the submission, the fierceness they
both inspired in her—was her life, and it was as real as her wet
pussy and hard nipples, as real as the crisp dollars the man had
given her.

"Be a good girl for Daddy, Tina," he said, then lifted her
up, carried her back to the chair, spread her across his lap and
spanked her extremely hard, over and over again. She could tell
he was spanking her faster than he ordinarily might have, and
she let the tears flow, let herself be a good girl and a bad girl,
a woman doing a friend a favor and a misbehaving daughter, a
woman who loved pain the way some women loved shoes and a
brat who'd misbehaved and needed punishing.

When he lifted her off his lap and placed her on the ground,
he kissed his fingers and pressed them to her lips. "Good-bye,

beautiful," he said, then reached into his pocket and pressed some more bills into her hand. It wasn't until she got home that she saw he'd also included a slip of paper with his phone number and one word: *Daddy*.

Taylor just shrugged as she sipped her iced coffee while Jesse asked her about her day. There'd been other men, but they'd seemed like children compared to him. "Oh, you saw Dylan, huh? He's a charmer. Hot, if you're into silver foxes." Jesse's voice was light, teasing, with no hint of the intensity Taylor had experienced. Taylor sipped her drink and smiled just as lightly. There was no reason to tell Jesse she had already called him and told him that Tina had crashed his sports car and needed him to pick her up at the mechanic's. He'd told her he'd meet her later, and that she was such a bad girl, he was going to focus on improving her behavior exclusively and let Janet fend for herself. Apparently, there were some things you couldn't find a substitute for, and Taylor didn't mind one bit.

ABOUT THE AUTHORS

JACQUELINE APPLEBEE (writing-in-shadows.co.uk) is a British writer who breaks down barriers with smut. Her stories have appeared in publications including *Best Women's Erotica, Best Lesbian Erotica, Penthouse* and *DIVA* magazine. Jacqueline hopes to write a best-selling novel so she can live in a lighthouse with a few adoring fans.

VIDA BAILEY is an occasional writer of erotica, living in Ireland. She has stories in Alison Tyler's *Love at First Sting* and Sommer Marsden's *Dirtyville*. More stories are soon to be published in Kristina Wright's *Steamlust* and Shanna Germain's *Bound by Lust* anthologies. You can find out more at heatsuffused.blogspot.com.

EMILY BINGHAM is a sex and food writer in Portland, Oregon. A connoisseur of words and exotic experiences, she has been published in *Best Bondage Erotica 2011* and various websites, including Cleansheets. Her adventures in the world of kinky rope fun can be found at her erotic writing blog queano-frope.com/.

KIKI DELOVELY (kikidelovely.wordpress.com) is a queer femme performer/writer whose work has appeared in *Best Lesbian Erotica 2011* and *2012, Take Me There: Transgender and Genderqueer Erotica,* and *Say Please: Lesbian BDSM Erotica.* Kiki's passions include artichokes, the Oxford comma, and taking on research for her writing.

ARIEL GRAHAM lives in Northern Nevada. Her work has appeared in several erotic anthologies and online sites such as Clean Sheets, Oysters & Chocolate and Fishnet.

JOY, also known as lyricalsongbird, has been an active participant in What It Is We Do for nine years and counting. She identifies as a female slave and takes pride in the service she offers to others. She writes from real-life experiences from her own personal journey.

ERRICA LIEKOS finally realized she could write about all the dirty things she likes to do in bed so long as she didn't use her own name. This is her first pseudonymous publication.

GINA MARIE lives, writes and dreams in the Pacific Northwest. She has authored erotic fiction for Clean Sheets, Oysters & Chocolate, *Lucrezia* Magazine, Sacchi Green's *Where the Girls Are* and Ily Goyanes's *Locker Room,* among others. She is also a published poet and photographer. She keeps a sexy blog at aphrodites-table.blogspot.com.

MAXINE MARSH draws her inspiration from the dark, sexy depths of horror, mythology and the kinky. Her erotica has been featured by Freaky Fountain Press, Vagabondage Press, Pill Hill Press, Oysters & Chocolate, and in *Seducing the Myth*, edited by Lucy Felthouse.

JADE MELISANDE lives in the Midwest with her two partners and one neurotic dog. A web designer by trade, she writes about her adventures as a kinky, bisexual, multi-partnered woman in her blog at piecesofjade.wordpress.com. She has previously published short erotica in anthologies such as *Orgasmic*, *Lesbian Lust* and *Power Play*.

GRAY MILLER is a writer and facilitator of "Unconferences" (called GRUEs) who travels around the world helping people explore their passions. He has worked as an educator and performer in the kink world for over a decade as "Graydancer," and currently blogs at LoveLifePractice.com.

TIFFANY REISZ is the author of *Seven Day Loan* (Spice Briefs) and *The Siren* (MIRA Books). Find her at tiffanyreisz.com.

Eroticist **GISELLE RENARDE** (wix.com/gisellerenarde/erotica) is a queer Canadian, avid volunteer, contributor to more than fifty short-story anthologies and author of dozens of electronic and print books, including *Anonymous, Ondine,* and *My Mistress' Thighs*.

COLE RILEY is the writer of several street classics: *Hot Snake Nights, Rough Trade, The Devil To Pay, The Killing Kind, Dark Blood Moon, Harlem Confidential* and *Guilty As Sin*. His writing has been featured in *Intimacy, Irresistible* and

Mammoth Book of Best New Erotica. He edited the collections *Too Much Boogie* and *Making The Hook-Up*.

TERESA NOELLE ROBERTS's short fiction has appeared in numerous anthologies, including *Best Bondage Erotica 2011 and 2012, Obsessed: Erotic Romance for Women* and *Kinky Girls*. She also writes erotic romances.

LORI SELKE lives in Oakland, California. More of her work can be found in *Ladies of the Bite* and the forthcoming *Demon Lovers: Succubi*. She is the mother of twin daughters and sometimes blogs about sex and parenting at Good Vibrations Magazine.

J. SINCLAIRE is a Toronto-based writer by profession but erotic by nature. Her work has appeared in anthologies such as *Lips Like Sugar, Got a Minute?* and *The Happy Birthday Book of Erotica*. A firm believer that sex and masturbation are both healthy and necessary, she considers it her civic duty to write smut. The rest is up to you.

KISSA STARLING writes in every genre and sensuality imaginable. She resides in the hot Southern state of Georgia with her family and numerous pets. Among her many vices are drive-in movies and lime-green bendy straws. To find out more about Kissa, and her writing, visit kissastarling.com.

BEX VANKOOT is a freelance writer of both erotica and nonfiction in the realm of love, sexuality, gender and spirituality. This passionate Canadian dakini dilettante, married pansexual and pagan polyamorist has always had a deep desire to change the world through the spread of sexual empowerment and alternative loving.

MOLLENA (MO) WILLIAMS (mollena.com) is a New Yorker, performer, BDSM educator and Executive Pervert. She is International Ms. Leather 2010 and Ms. SF Leather 2009. Consciously kinky since 1993, active in Leather and BDSM since 1996, she authored *The Toybag Guide: Taboo Play* and coauthored *Playing Well With Others* with Lee Harrington.

KRISTINA WRIGHT (kristinawright.com) is a full-time writer and the editor of several Cleis Press anthologies including *Fairy Tale Lust, Dream Lover, Steamlust, Best Erotic Romance* and *Lustfully Ever After.* She lives in Virginia with her husband and two young sons and spends a lot of time in coffee shops.

ABOUT
THE EDITOR

RACHEL KRAMER BUSSEL (rachelkramerbussel.com) is a
New York–based author, editor and blogger. She has edited
over forty books of erotica, including *Anything for You; Suite
Encounters; Going Down; Irresistible; Best Bondage Erotica
2011, 2012* and *2013; Gotta Have It; Obsessed; Women in
Lust; Surrender; Orgasmic; Bottoms Up: Spanking Good
Stories; Spanked: Red-Cheeked Erotica; Naughty Spanking
Stories from A to Z 1* and *2; Fast Girls; Smooth; Passion; The
Mile High Club; Do Not Disturb; Tasting Him; Tasting Her;
Please, Sir; Please, Ma'am; He's on Top; She's on Top; Caught
Looking; Hide and Seek; Crossdressing; Rubber Sex; Only
You;* and *Twice the Pleasure.* She is *Best Sex Writing* series
editor, and winner of 8 IPPY (Independent Publisher) Awards.
Her work has been published in over one hundred antholo-
gies, including *Best American Erotica 2004* and *2006; Zane's
Z-Rated, Chocolate Flava 2* and *Purple Panties; Everything
You Know About Sex Is Wrong; Single State of the Union* and

Desire: Women Write About Wanting. She wrote the popular "Lusty Lady" column for the *Village Voice.*

Rachel has written for *AVN, Bust,* Cleansheets.com, *Cosmopolitan, Curve,* The Daily Beast, Fresh Yarn, TheFrisky.com, *Glamour,* Gothamist, Huffington Post, *Inked,* Nerve, Mediabistro, *Newsday, New York Post, Penthouse, Playgirl, Radar,* The Root, Salon, *San Francisco Chronicle, Time Out New York* and *Zink,* among others. She has appeared on "The Gayle King Show," "The Martha Stewart Show," "The Berman and Berman Show," NY1 and Showtime's "Family Business." She hosted the popular In the Flesh Erotic Reading Series (inthefleshreadingseries.com), featuring readers from Susie Bright to Zane, and speaks at conferences, does readings and teaches erotic writing workshops across the country. She blogs at lustylady.blogspot.com.

More from Rachel Kramer Bussel

Do Not Disturb
Hotel Sex Stories
Edited by Rachel Kramer Bussel

A delicious array of hotel hookups where it seems like anything can happen—and quite often does. "If *Do Not Disturb* were a hotel, it would be a 5-star hotel with the luxury of 24/7 entertainment available."—Erotica Revealed
978-1-57344-344-9 $14.95

Bottoms Up
Spanking Good Stories
Edited by Rachel Kramer Bussel

As sweet as it is kinky, *Bottoms Up* will propel you to pick up a paddle and share in both pleasure and pain, or perhaps simply turn the other cheek.
ISBN 978-1-57344-362-3 $15.95

Orgasmic
Erotica for Women
Edited by Rachel Kramer Bussel

What gets you off? Let *Orgasmic* count the ways...with 25 stories focused on female orgasm, there is something here for every reader.
ISBN 978-1-57344-402-6 $14.95

Please, Sir
Erotic Stories of Female Submission
Edited by Rachel Kramer Bussel

These 22 kinky stories celebrate the thrill of submission by women who know exactly what they want.
ISBN 978-1-57344-389-0 $14.95

Fast Girls
Erotica for Women
Edited by Rachel Kramer Bussel

Fast Girls celebrates the girl with a reputation, the girl who goes all the way, and the girl who doesn't know how to say "no."
ISBN 978-1-57344-384-5 $14.95

Many More Than Fifty Shades of Erotica

Unleash Your Favorite Fantasies

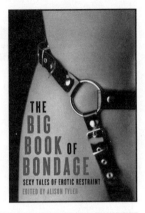

Ordering is easy! Call us toll free or fax us to place your MC/VISA order.
You can also mail the order form below with payment to:
Cleis Press, 2246 Sixth St., Berkeley, CA 94710.

ORDER FORM

QTY	TITLE	PRICE

SUBTOTAL _____

SHIPPING _____

SALES TAX _____

TOTAL _____

Add $3.95 postage/handling for the first book ordered and $1.00 for each additional
book. Outside North America, please contact us for shipping rates. California residents
add 9% sales tax. Payment in U.S. dollars only.

* Free book of equal or lesser value. Shipping and applicable sales tax extra.

Cleis Press • Phone: (800) 780-2279 • Fax: (510) 845-8001
orders@cleispress.com • www.cleispress.com
You'll find more great books on our website

Follow us on Twitter @cleispress • Friend/fan us on Facebook